Alternate

Consequence

Judith Fabris

Trade Paperback

@Copyright 2021

All Rights Reserved

Library of Congress: 1-10187955411

ISBN: 978-0-9969593-8-4

Requests for information should be addressed to:

A Vegas Publisher, LLC.

www.vegaspublishers.com

vegaspublisher@gmail.com

First edition: 2021

Friendship isn't how long you know someone. It's about who walks into your life, says I'm here for you and then proves it.

-Nicholas Sparks

To my friends who have been a constant source of support.

Cast of Characters

Penelope Maud Wells, Penny - heiress, art curator, philanthropist

William Tennent - Penny Well's life-long nemesis

Lavinia Colchester Troyer - Penny's cousin, married to Dr. Michel Troyer and Jean-Luc's twin brother

Jean-Luc Troyer - art consultant and Penny's confidant

Trudy King - Penny's and Lavinia's long-time friend

Ursula Becker - cook, house manager, and friend of Trudy

Dr. Lottie Wasserman - owner of Driscoll Painting and dear friend of Ernst Weber

Ernst Weber - retrieved painting from the Nazis, belonging to Wasserman family; spirited Lottie out of Germany as a young child at the beginning of World War II

Aisalynn Sheperd- young violinist and grandniece of Ernst Weber

Max Dedham - detective Laguna Police Department

Harley Brosnan - senior detective Los Angeles Police Department.

1

Penny Wells curled her long, slender legs on the large comfy couch. Her bare toes, manicured in fire engine red, peeked out from under her chartreuse linen caftan. She was enjoying the afternoon with her best friend, Trudy King. The house manager, Ursula, brought in a crystal bowl filled with fresh fruit for the ladies to enjoy. The two friends spoke in whispers, trying not to disturb Lynn as she practiced in another room. The striking violinist pulled her coal-black hair into a tight tail to avoid getting it caught in the strings.

As a young child, everyone called her by her formal name, Aisalynn. During her college years, she preferred a less formal version, Lynn.

"She's exceptional, isn't she, Trudy?"

"Yes, she is. She'll be a solo violinist with the Minneapolis Symphony for a concert at the Segerstrom in June."

"Trudy, I almost forgot. I brought a letter from Vie

Lee. It's in my purse; let me get it. I knew you would enjoy reading it."

"I think about her often. You have a lovely reading voice. Read it, please."

Dear Penny,

How are you? Sean and I are enjoying an easy retirement life. The beach, walking, and some fun road trips are just a few of our favorite activities. We went to South Carolina recently. What a beautiful state.

In the letter you sent, you mentioned you were in the throes of a divorce. I'm so sorry. I hope life is treating you much better now.

My letter's main reason is that Sean received a police notification that Bill Tennent is scheduled to be released from prison soon. No specific date was provided, but you might want to call the Department of Corrections and find out. If they don't want to offer you information, go to the police department and ask them. You are entitled to know.

Tennent's anger may have increased over time and the last thing I would want would be for that maniac to try to hurt you or the gallery. You might also want to call

Avery Tennent at his gallery to see if you can get more
information.

I don't want to worry you, but I want to keep you
safe. I miss seeing you. We had some great times. Now
that my detective days are over, Sean and I spend the late
afternoons talking and sipping some wonderful rum
concoctions while watching the sunset. Can't you bring an
exhibit to Florida and come visit? Please tell Vinnie and
Trudy hello for me.
Much love,
Vie Lee
(and a big hug too)

Penny had been spending the weekend at Hilltop, Trudy's
home that Penny's father had designed the year before he
suddenly passed away. The views of the coastline were
breathtaking. Penny had told him it was the best piece of
architecture he had ever designed.

"Oh, no!" said Trudy. "You mean we aren't
permanently rid of that pest?"

"Who's a pest?" Lynn had her violin tucked under
her arm as she joined Trudy and Penny in the living room.

She was all ears to the conversation.

"Bill Tennent." Penny and Trudy chorused.

"Who is he?"

Penny began, "He was one of the worst experiences of my life. I had been a curator and managing director of the Driscoll Museum in Washington, D.C. Jean-Luc's father was the Jeu de Paume curator in Paris. He invited me to curate a retrospective of Maud Driscoll paintings. She was my grandmother and one of the most famous artists of her time."

"I know. I admired her painting at the Legacy Gallery. It was enclosed in a large display box."

"Under lock and key, and the box is wired with an alarm system. Since I can't be in Laguna full-time, Trudy manages the gallery for me. The original name for the gallery was la Galerie de l'Heritage. Over the years it has become referred to as the English counterpart, Legacy Gallery. I think people might have had some difficulty in pronouncing the name."

"Well, it's a beautiful gallery, whatever the name. Please tell me more."

"Thank you, Lynn. To continue my saga, and it is one," Penny laughed. "When I was traveling to the Jeu de

Paume with the collection to go on display, a Driscoll painting was stolen mid-flight. Tennent appeared at the museum in Paris posing as an insurance appraiser for the Driscoll Museum. I am familiar with many people in the industry, yet I had never met or seen him before. He accused me of being the thief. An investigation discovered he had the canvas stolen for himself to sell to a Chinese buyer. For over a year, he was relentless in hounding me with repeated attempts to ruin my career and reputation. It was a nightmare! None of the museums would consider scheduling an interview with me. It was a terrible black mark on whatever I wanted to do.

"Even Jean-Luc's father, with all his international museum connections, was unable to help me. I went through hell restoring my reputation and getting the painting back.

"I opened the gallery to earn an income, my own income, and I didn't want to ask my parents for help. Tennent planned another theft of a different Driscoll masterpiece, and he nearly succeeded. He has seen the inside California's prisons since then.

"Years have passed without any news about him other than he was incarcerated. It has been nice living without fear. Maybe I should hire another bodyguard by the time he is released. He is a psychopath, a very dangerous man."

"It's sad when you think about it," said Trudy. "He came from a kind and loving family and had a world of opportunity for success. Jean-Luc will be here at cocktail time, and we will let him know about Tennent. He will find out more for you."

"In the meantime, Lynn, would you play a piece for me?" Penny changed from her position to one where she sat and could reach the fruit with ease. Selecting an apricot, she smiled at everyone. "Truly, this is my downfall!" Everyone around her giggled at her comment and reached for fruit too. Penny had added a few pounds every year. Now she couldn't be called fat, only pleasingly plump. Even though a miserable cook, she could eat like an athlete and loved to feast on Ursula's strudel and other fattening delights.

Lynn poised her violin in the crook of her left arm. She began a stirring crescendo of the concerto she was rehearsing. An accomplished artist at the age of twenty-six, she diligently practiced for the Costa Mesa Segerstrom Center concert. The melodic sounds she brought from her violin resounded throughout Trudy's home.

Lynn was Ernst Weber's great-grandniece, a distant relative Ernst thought he would never have the opportunity to meet. She brought him so much happiness in the short time they spent together. As beautiful on the outside, she was inside, just like her uncle. He adored listening to Lynn play.

Concentrating on her bow, her shiny black ponytail flopped from side to side like the waves seen crashing on the coastline below Hilltop. Five years prior, the petite young musician graduated from the U.S.C. School of Music at the top of her class.

Once she came to live at Trudy's, her Uncle Ernst's best friend in Laguna Beach, she religiously drove to Long Beach each week to continue her violin lessons from Camilla Wickes. Her teacher was quick to point out that when she was the same age, the world considered her a violin virtuoso. Lynn aspired to be famous like her teacher.

The unexpected ring of the doorbell interrupted Lynn's concert.

2

A special delivery envelope arrived with Lynn's birth name on it, Ayslynn. She looked at the envelope with curiosity, tore it open, and read the message aloud. The envelope's contents left her trembling with the news.

HARRISON GREEN AND WORLEY

Attorneys at Law

23657 West Green Street

Pasadena, CA 91103

626-431-5555

March 23, 2001

Re: The Estate of Ernst Weber

Miss Aisalynn M. Sheperd

c/o Mrs. Gertrude King

617 Hilltop Drive

Laguna Beach, CA 92652

Dear Miss Sheperd,

We represent the estate of the late Ernst Weber. This office is seeking to determine if you are the sole survivor under the terms of his will. Would you please contact this office at your earliest convenience so we can arrange a meeting and confirm you are the Aisalynn Sheperd we are seeking, great-grandniece of the late Mr. Ernst Weber. We would be happy to meet in Laguna Beach if it is more convenient for you.

Yours very truly,

Thomas Worley

HARRISON GREEN AND WORLEY

Trudy made a silent gasp as she listened to Lynn read the letter aloud. She knew the tremendous fortune Lynn would be inheriting. "Had the Nazis taken it all? Had the Russians ransacked the house?" She could not wait to find out more.

Trudy had been the one who encouraged Ernst to come to the United States and had been instrumental in helping him find a way to reach his life-long destination.

Trudy embraced Lynn and began to cry.

"Oh honey, I've been inside that home many times. It is huge; some say the size of a castle. Even Penny has been there. One time we snuck her into East Germany for a day. She posed as Ursula and used her papers. It's a wonder we weren't caught and sent to prison. We were quite adventurous, just a few years older than you are now. It was a dangerous time to cross into East Germany as we did. The wall was a formidable iron curtain and very scary."

"What would I ever do with a place that size?"

"I'm not certain you would want to do anything but sell it. The 'Haus du Violine' is a magnificent treasure."

"Why is it called that?" Uncle Ernst didn't play an instrument, did he?"

"I'm going to let Ursula tell that story during lunch. It will make for great conversation. But before you decide anything, you must visit the property and explore every inch. Uncle Ernst led an accomplished life, many acts against the Nazi regime. He repatriated numerous paintings and other items of value taken from Jewish families. You cannot consider selling the property until you have searched in every nook and cranny, look under every floorboard. Penny, if you aren't too busy curating a new exhibit at the Los Angeles County Museum of Art, perhaps you may want to accompany Lynn."

"I'd love to," said Penny. "But can it wait until July when I get my vacation?"

"We should speak with the attorney. Why don't you call Mr. Worley and invite him here for a luncheon meeting? Then we all can decide what your next course of action should be."

Arrangements were made for Mr. Worley to arrive at Hilltop the following Wednesday for lunch. Ursula's kitchen smelled like an Italian trattoria. She prepared a pasta primavera, her special homemade garlic bread, a leafy green salad with avocado, deep-fried onion rings, followed by tiramisu for dessert.

"No wine, Ursula, just iced tea with lemon. This is an important meeting for Lynn."

"Wow! Ursula, you're incredible," said Lynn as she dipped a teaspoon into the sauce. "You've conquered a whole other country's cuisine in our kitchen. It tastes divine."

Ursula smiled, knowing her cooking brought joy to all those she served. She continued to spread butter on the bread for toasting. She topped the bread with grated Parmesan and added a dash of paprika when the doorbell rang.

Lynn watched Trudy stop at the mirror in the foyer to check her hair before answering the door.

"Mr. Worley, I'm Trudy King. Won't you please come in?"

Tom outstretched his arm to shake hands with her. At that moment, Aisalynn arrived to greet him also. "Hello, Mr. Worley, I'm Aisalynn. My friends call me Lynn."

"Hello, I'm Tom." Their eyes met. "It's so nice to meet you. Thank you for inviting me here. Much nicer than a stuffy office. Don't you agree?"

Not typically tongue-tied, she answered a soft, "Yes." Tom Worley probably wasn't more than two years older than Lynn. *I wonder if he is married. He's so charming and handsome. Look at those dimples!*

She ushered the young lawyer into the living room, making introductions. Trudy smiled at him and looked at

Lynn. *You're smitten, young lady. I already introduced myself at the door.* "Tom, will you please sit down and make yourself comfortable. Would you like a glass of iced tea?"

"Sounds great. Let's get some business taken care of first, so I can have a few minutes to enjoy the day." He turned to look out the window, admiring the view. "Lynn, how do you know you're related to Ernst Weber?"

Trudy urged Lynn. "Go ahead, tell him, honey."

"My Uncle Ernst, whom I met only about two years ago, was the youngest brother of my mother's grandmother. Before the First World War, my great-grandmother left Germany at the age of sixteen to come to America. Ernst would barely have been walking at that time. She arrived in Wyoming, took a job teaching at an elementary school. After the war, she wrote back to her German relatives to receive her inheritance and was told it would cost more to mail than what she would inherit because of German marks' devaluation. That was the last time she heard from anyone in her family. Estranged and alone, she traveled to Southern California and moved to Los Angeles, where she met my great-grandfather. I never met him; he died before I was born. My great-

21

grandmother gave my mother a list of all her relatives in Germany and a few known addresses. My Oma never saw her brother. She died before he came to the United States."

"That's so sad. So how did your mother find Ernst?" The young woman and her story captivated Tom.

"My mother had the curiosity of a cat." Lynn laughed. "After the Second World War ended and correspondence was being received, she sent a letter to the house where Ernst lived, addressed it to the current occupant. In the letter, she told the recipient who she was and that her grandmother had a much younger brother named Ernst. By any chance, would he still be alive? Ernst was ecstatic to hear from her, and within a month, she had his reply. It was his hope that he could someday find a way to come to the United States.

"Three years later, Trudy brought him to our doorstep in North Hollywood. Unfortunately, my mother, his cousin, had passed away two months before his arrival. Since I was now alone, dear Trudy invited me to come live with her. We're not related, but she's the closest anyone could be to me and not be a mother. That's how Uncle Ernst and I are related."

"Mr. Weber told my father the same story when he

came to our office to have his will drawn. It's all recorded in an office memorandum." Tom put on his most lawyer-like demeanor. "Lynn, your uncle bequeathed to you his home in East Berlin and all the contents remaining inside."

Trudy gasped audibly. She knew what Ernst had left behind. No one had lived in his home since he left for the United States. She wondered if the premises had been left intact or if vandals had ransacked it.

"I will need to go there, Lynn. I wish Thornton were still alive," Trudy said. "He could be of so much help. Because of this damned arthritis, I'm not thrilled to travel to Germany during the cold months. It has to be during the summer; otherwise, I can't go. Can you wait until mid-July to travel to Germany?"

"That would be perfect because my appearances are over the end of June."

"Lynn, honey, you're going to need to spend time in East Berlin to comprehend the true value of this inheritance. The countless rooms hold many treasures. Ernst was quite clever and hid the most valuable items in secret compartments. I remember huge stacks of paintings leaning against the walls. Why don't you ask Jean-Luc to go? He might want to come with his partner Adrian. They are well connected, and both know art and art values. Jean-Luc also speaks some German. I know he is well acquainted with gallery owners and museum directors around the world."

Tom interrupted. "Trudy, my firm told me I could go on what we're calling an 'expedition.'" He used finger quotations in emphasis.

"It sounds like this will be the treasure hunt of a lifetime. I'm grateful your firm will let you accompany me. We'll talk with Jean-Luc today, Trudy. "

"Lynnie, thank you for saying you will wait until mid-summer. Even then, that house feels like one is in the middle of an ice storm. Ernst had fires burning in the hearths year-round. You will need a passport, and you'll definitely need some warm clothes if you plan to spend time in the house. The only place we can get you a passport is in Los Angeles. Maybe, we can buy luggage for you while we are there.

"Lunch is ready. Lynn will lead the way to the dining room. I hope you like Italian."

"One of my favorites." Tom, the consummate gentleman, held out a chair for Trudy. Then he did the same for Lynn.

The conversation was a bit awkward at first, and then became non-stop between the attorney and the violinist.

"Where's your father, Lynn?" Tom asked as he took another bite of the pasta.

"I never knew him. He died in an unfortunate electrical accident when I was an infant."

"Frightful." Tom looked at her. "Well, where did you grow up then?" Tom looked at Trudy and asked for another helping of salad. "This food is scrumptious."

Lynn smiled at him, then continued with her story. "Glendale, most of my life. I had an apartment near college, but when Mother became ill, I moved in with her to take care of her. I was able to relieve the caregiver who spent most days with her."

"Did you ever get a vacation? Did your mother ever hear you in concert?"

"I don't think I know what a vacation is, but the caregiver brought my mother to a couple of my local concerts. She was absolutely thrilled and would hum the music for days afterward. I think those were some of her happiest moments."

"I'd love to hear you play."

"Lynnie, so would I." Trudy chimed in. "Will you give us a concert after we finish our dessert."

"My pleasure."

"Tom, why has it taken your firm so long to locate Lynn?" Protective of her ward, Trudy eagerly awaited his answer.

"I don't know that answer. My father also died a couple of years ago. I just passed the bar and became an associate last August. It looks like someone dropped the ball on this case, but I don't know who. Perhaps my office discovered Lynn was not easy to locate. I can only apologize for the delay. But I'm so glad we found you, Lynn."

Ursula brought in the tiramisu and more iced tea. "May I come and listen too?"

"Of course, Ursula," said Trudy. "You're part of the family."

"Lynn, could you play something by Mahler?" Ursula requested. "Did I ever tell you when I worked for Ernst, a frightened young woman came to see him late one night? She clutched her violin case and slipped into the house. I recall your uncle saying she was related to Gustav

Mahler. She left empty-handed, leaving her precious instrument with your uncle. After that visit, I never saw her again.

"When the construction of the wall began, Ernst insisted I go and stay with Trudy in West Berlin. We were much younger then, weren't we, dear? I managed the house and whatever else was needed. I never returned to East Berlin. It was the best day when Ernst arrived here at Hilltop. I miss him terribly."

"You certainly have a story of your own, Ursula." Tom smiled at her. "Your English is fluent, and your cooking is simply divine."

"She is the jewel of this family. I don't know what I would do without her. She is the dearest of friends." Ursula beamed at Trudy's comment.

Lynn picked up her violin. "Ursula, just for you, part of Mahler's 4th Symphony." Glorious music filled the house, and when she finished, her audience of three clapped and clapped.

"Bravo! You're wonderful, Lynn." Tom clapped more.

Trudy observed the two of them. *Sparks are flying!*

"I'm playing a concert at the Segerstrom. We'd love to have you join us and come to the small after-party."

"Sounds wonderful, Lynn. As much as I hate to say it, I must return to my office. Thank you for a delightful afternoon ladies, we will be in touch soon."

Tom walked to his car without his feet touching the ground. At least that was how he felt.

3

"Trudy, do you still plan to accompany me to Germany?"

"Not for the entire time I expect you will be there. I must first go to Texas and make certain everything is okay at Thornton's ranch. Since his death two years ago, I haven't made any decisions about what I'm going to do with all that property. Everyone who worked for him is getting on in years, too, and I don't know how much longer they can continue. I don't want to live in Texas. I have the gallery and all the tenants in the complex to manage, even though I have a good manager. I think it would be in your best interest to have Penny accompany you. Penny, would you like a couple of overnight houseguests? We can talk more about Lynn's trip. Will that fit into your plans?"

"I'd love to see your new condo. I heard you say it's on the parade route. Next year, I would love to watch the Rose Parade and stay there overnight. Please say yes to our request. Maybe we can ask Tom to join us so we can all spend more time getting to know him."

Trudy smiled to herself. *I think you just want to see Tom, young lady.* "I can't decide whether the flowers in Laguna or the flowers in Pasadena are more beautiful."

"Oh, Trudy, they are all different flowers. You are so funny." Lynn loved the chance to tease her guardian.

"Penny, it's always too long between visits, even if I saw you a few days ago." Trudy hugged her good friend.

"I know it has. Have you talked with Vinnie lately?"

"She came down to visit with the youngest grandchild, and Lynn babysat while we went out to lunch," said Trudy. "She looks wonderful. Her hair has silver highlights in it now. I intend on keeping mine blonde, and it looks like you want to remain a redhead forever." She twirled a lock of Penny's hair. "I received another note from Vie Lee. Let me get it."

Dear Penny,
Sean received word that Tennent will be released from prison in fourteen days. Please take extra special care. We love you,
Vie Lee

4

"Penny?" Lynn looked at both women. "I would think that after all this time in prison, Tennent might want to do something constructive, to rehabilitate."

"Not this man. If he had been able to do something from his cell, he would. He wants to harass me and cause problems, even after all these years. I think it's part of his vindictive personality. In Paris, and right to his face, I might add, I told Vinnie if she wanted to go out to dinner with Bill Tennent or date him, to be my guest; I wanted nothing to do with him. He doesn't let go of anything. We were only in our late twenties at that time. How can someone hold a grudge for that long? It's beyond comprehension and such a waste of constructive energy."

"Trudy, contact Jean-Luc as soon as you return to Hilltop. He needs to be informed."

"Penny, I want to make sure you will be able to accompany me to Berlin. The thought of inheriting Uncle Ernst's castle is daunting. At least that is how everyone seems to describe it and the contents. Since Uncle Ernst and you were responsible for returning so many artifacts and paintings to their rightful heirs, it seemed only natural to ask you to curate everything, lock, stock, and barrel." Lynn grinned at her last comment. "Trudy said she could only come for a couple of weeks and that I shouldn't go until mid -July. What do you think? "

"Lynn, I'd be absolutely honored to help. If we find historical art and artifacts, may I have Los Angeles County Museum of Art do a retrospective?"

"Of course, Penny. What a brilliant idea. I hope we find heirs, and whatever we are not able to reclaim, I'd like to sell and donate."

"Let's see what we uncover first."

"You have inherited quite a bit of responsibility. I will pour iced tea, and let's sit on the patio. We have much to discuss."

"It's amazing to me Ernst found you." Penny's face glowed as she realized what a wonderful gift Lynn had given her to curate for the museum.

"I'd love to go with you and see what treasures are inside Ernst's castle." Penny smiled at Lynn. "July will be a perfect time to go because I will have my well-earned vacation."

" And July would be great because I will be finished with performances until the fall."

"Do you think Jean-Luc would like to go?"

"He would be an asset, and he loves adventures. Anyone else you think might be helpful? Trudy told me Uncle Ernst could have left many paintings and artifacts hidden in the walls, under the floorboards, even in the attic. She said that before I even thought about selling, I should check everywhere."

"Smart lady."

"Maybe that violin Ursula told us about is hidden in one of the walls."

"An exciting prospect, Lynn. We'll get it all together. Okay with you?"

"Just wonderful, Penny. Thank you. This has truly been an exciting day for me. I want you to meet Tom. May I call and ask him to dinner?"

"Of course, honey," said Penny. Tell him to meet us at the Chronicle at 7 pm. I'll call and make a reservation now."

5

Trudy, Jean-Luc, and Penny held a three-way phone conversation. "Lynn said she can't handle anything except violin practice and concerts right now. She gave me express permission to do whatever would be necessary regarding the artwork and house." Trudy announced at the beginning of the call.

"Before we begin," said Jean-Luc, "I just received a letter from the California Department of Corrections. Bill Tennent is being released at the end of May."

"Well, it's not like we haven't been forewarned. First, the two letters from Vie Lee, and now you received a letter. Oh lord, are we going to have to put up with him again? I thought he'd be gone forever." Jean-Luc and Trudy could hear the angst in Penny's voice.

"Don't worry, Penny. He is as old as we are. He's not going to be around like he was," said Jean-Luc.

"He's going to show up at the L'Heritage Gallery. Just wait." Penny's face drained of color.

"We'll put a guard on duty if you'd like. I'll see to it, Penny." Jean-Luc comforted her. "We won't let anything happen to you or a Driscoll painting. Or to Trudy, for that matter, since she is the manager."

"Well, now we have the good news with the bad. We need a full meeting with everyone," said Trudy. "It's probably easier to hold it at Vinnie's and Michel's. I'll plan it if that is okay with you. Today is Thursday. Lynn needs to practice for her upcoming concert. We could schedule a meeting on Sunday afternoon if that works for everyone."

"That should work well. I'll ask Vinnie if I can use her guestroom. I haven't seen her in much too long a time. We are all so caught up in our own lives. And I thought the reason you came to Pasadena was to see me because you missed me."

"All right, Penny, I get your sarcasm." Trudy laughed along with Jean-Luc.

6

Vinnie loved having everyone visit their home on Harbor Isle. Sundays were special days because Michel usually had the day free. Trudy, Lynn, and Jean-Luc were the first to arrive. Penny arrived a few minutes later, toting her suitcase.

The dining room table was informally set with platters of cold roast beef, ham, and cheeses. Different types of fresh-baked bread were plattered, including sourdough, rye with caraway seeds, and multi-grain. A variety of condiments and fixings filled the table's center: mayonnaise, lettuce, sliced tomatoes, horseradish, cornichons, large black olives, sweet pickles, Dijon mustard, ketchup, potato salad, three-bean salad, a pasta salad, deviled eggs, and a mixed green salad. A big pitcher of iced tea topped with lemon slices, bottles of red and white wine, and a platter of chocolate eclairs for dessert rounded out the luncheon display.

"Vinnie, that table is humongous. There's enough food to feed two armies. It all looks more than wonderful, but we're only five normal eaters." Penny shook her head at her cousin. Entertaining her friends was one of the highlights of Vinnie's life. Penny reflected on years before when Vinnie lost her first husband and children in a fatal traffic accident. She was so thrilled to witness her best friend and cousin living a happy, contented life. She and Michel were well suited for each other. Penny smiled inwardly, *I'm a good matchmaker.*

"I just didn't want anyone to go hungry." She gave Penny's arm a warm squeeze.

"You never would, cousin dear,"

Everyone gathered around the table with a plate in hand, ready to eat. After lunch and playful conversation, Penny asked everyone, "Would you all gather in the sunroom where the couches are comfortable, and if wine spilled on the floor, it would be easy to clean."

"Penny, are you saying my house is uncomfortable?" Vinnie looked at her cousin askance.

"Of course not, Vinnie. I just don't want to see anything spilled on your beautiful carpets. Our conversation may become a little heated after I read this letter from Vie Lee."

"I wondered why you were so secretive," said Vinnie. "Read the letter, cousin. I'm all ears."

Penny also read Lynn's inheritance letter from the law firm. Once Penny finished the letters, the room was abuzz with conversation.

"Whoa, everyone." Trudy led the conversation. "Let me tell you what has been decided so far. Lynn said she couldn't plan or think about going to Berlin until her concert season finishes. That is the end of June. In July, she is going to East Berlin when Penny has her vacation from the Los Angeles County Museum of Art. Because Lynn is permitting Penny to curate a show at the museum, they will give Penny extra time to coordinate everything. That means she may be gone for more than two weeks. I'd like Jean-Luc to come with us if he can.

"Remember, I need to go to Texas to check on the Thornton holdings first and will be arriving in Berlin after everyone else.

"I told Lynn that Ernst likely left many extraordinary paintings he repatriated from the Nazis. Ursula told us also about a violin. I've never seen it, but he listened to concerts performed by a violinist who died at Auschwitz.

"We probably should have had Lynn here, but she asked me to handle everything because all she wants to do is practice. She trusts our decisions. I didn't want her to become frightened when I tell you what I know."

"Don't keep us in suspense, Trudy. What are you hiding?" Jean-Luc peppered her with questions.

"When Ernst left his home in Berlin, he touched nothing on the walls. He asked his property caretaker to manage everything. If for some reason he never returned, they could live there until Ernst's relatives were found. I know he must have had a lawyer overseeing the estate because the property is so vast, with huge gardens and so on. I just hope 'Haus du Violine' is still standing and hasn't been destroyed."

Penny was quick to ask another question. "Do you think the caretakers would still be living on the property?"

"I have no idea. I think it would be prudent to have German representation also. Tom's firm, I'm confident, could find someone to act on their behalf."

"That is wise," said Penny. "I hope they have not walked off with everything on the walls and in the cupboards."

"It's my feeling if the house remained intact, then we could offer them a picture or two, they could sell them and receive a nice sum, or we could just offer them money," said Trudy. "Lynn doesn't have any money yet from the inheritance," Trudy continued, "I'll be happy to supply all the funds upfront, and she can repay me when she can. I'll talk with her tonight."

"Even if it is only the physical property remaining and nothing inside, the palatial estate will be worth a lot. East Berlin is booming. Adrian was in Berlin last month and said so many new international brand hotels were open and a plethora of fine restaurants to choose from," said Jean-Luc. "Maybe the violin is still there?"

"I told Lynn she must go through every closet, floorboard, wall, and whatever or wherever there might be a possible hiding place," said Trudy. "It's obvious she won't want to live there but sell the property as a hotel or other commercial enterprise."

"Trudy, you've got to go with Lynn. You even speak the language." Michel was quick to point out.

"Find someone to manage the gallery while you are gone," Jean-Luc said. "We will probably be in Germany at least a month. Come and meet us there."

"Trudy, it will be great to have you come on this expedition. That is what I'm calling it," said Penny.

"Penny, do you think it might be possible to find an art student who might like a summer job? I could offer whomever room and board since Ursula will be at the house. Whoever it is must be thoroughly vetted- no dogs, cats, smoking, and I'm hiding all the liquor." Everyone laughed at Trudy's last remark but agreed with her wholeheartedly.

"Lavinia, darling," said her husband, "I think you not only managed a lovely lunch but were responsible for putting together a search party. I would love for us to join them. It sounds like great fun, even though it will be a lot of work."

"If you have got even ten days free time, come and join us. It would be fun to work alongside my brother after so many years." Jean-Luc said.

"Guys, it's been great fun seeing you all, but hospital duties are calling me, even on my day off," Michel said as he stood. "I hope I can get enough time off to go on this big adventure. Let's see what I can figure out. Maybe we can."

"Talk at you later, bro." Jean-Luc cuffed his twin

on the back of his head, just like when they were kids.

Penny asked for quiet from everyone. "Now we have another potential problem to discuss. I don't know if Tennent has any money. He must be in his late sixties or early seventies, but he probably has more body strength than any of us from pumping iron at the prison. He certainly doesn't appear to have any leanings toward book reading."

"You're right, Jean-Luc. I think Penny should hire a bodyguard," Michel shouted as he was leaving the house. "Trudy," the doctor added, "should put security in the complex and around the gallery. Maybe you could put in an electronic gate at Hilltop so no one could come onto the premises."

Trudy nodded her head. "That's a good idea. I'll call a gate company tomorrow."

"Penny, how is the security at your condo complex?" Jean-Luc asked.

"Two gates in front, both locked with only my phone to open them. In the back to the patio, he'd have to climb two floors on a ladder from the parking lot, also locked."

"Sounds like you're pretty well protected from the

inside. I worry about you at the museum. Who watches you there?" Jean-Luc asked.

"Maybe I can pay for an extra security person. I don't want to draw attention to myself or be alarming to patrons and employees while roaming the gallery halls."

7

Tennent shaded his eyes from the hot sun as he walked through the prison gate. He couldn't walk fast enough toward the man waiting for him in the dark green four-door sedan.

"Deke, Deke, my man, it's so good to see a friend. I'm so glad to get out of this hell hole. Where are we going?"

"Los Angeles, that's where I have my apartment."

"I need some clothes. This garbage they gave me, I can't wait to get out of them."

"No problem, boss, there are discount stores and thrift shops we can hit."

"I haven't touched my bank account in years. I don't know if I have any money left."

"Don't worry if you don't. I can stake you. The ponies have been pretty good to me lately."

"I don't want to go into the bank until I have some decent clothes. Need to make that good impression, ya know. I'm going to say I've been out of the country and out of contact. I want to go to a branch I've never been in before."

"Not hard. There's a Bank of America on every corner almost. That and a Starbucks."

"Starbucks, that's something new. What is it?"

"A place to get fancy coffee. I'll take you there."

"Thanks, but not in these duds."

After two hours on the road, Deke pulled into a parking place in front of Van Nuys Boulevard's four-plex. "We're here."

He unlocked his front door and invited the newly released felon inside. "Only one bathroom, but we each will have a bedroom. There's a Goodwill around the corner. We can walk there and find you a pair of jeans or khaki pants and a polo shirt. Probably cost about $5.00. Then we will go get something to eat."

"Oh, man, I can't tell you how good this hamburger tastes." Tennent wiped juices off his chin. "And the fries. Manna from heaven. The food in the joint can't be called food. I asked to work in the kitchen, thinking I might improve the food. Not so. It's a good reason to stay out of prison."

The two men walked back to Deke's apartment and chilled out over a few beers.

"Do you know where that bitch Wells is? I sure cooked her bacon for a while there." Tennent's smile had a lascivious turn.

"She is a senior curator now at the Los Angeles County Art Museum. She got married a few years ago, but the papers recently said she was divorced. I recognized her face in a society picture."

"What are you doing reading that trash?"

"Couldn't help to see it. It was on the front page."

"Deke, as sure as I'm sitting here, I'm going to find her and kill her. Thought about it every day in the pen."

"But then you'll be going back. Why do that dude?"

"I have a beautiful plan, and before they find her body, I'll be long gone outta the country."

"I don't want you to ask me to do anything. I've been trying to stay straight and clean. I just finished my time with my parole officer. I want to die of old age on the outside, boss."

"No problem. I'll find myself a place to live, so there will be no connection to you."

"Thanks for understanding, pal."

Once Tennent got situated, he checked his bank account balance and acquired a couple of credit cards. He wasted no time utilizing all the knowledge he acquired in prison. Not able to help himself, he bought a vintage Cadillac and drove to Best Buy to buy a laptop computer. He felt like he was back in business. At his apartment, he set up his new purchase on his kitchen table and went to work. "The joint did teach me how to find my way around computers." Excited that he now had the internet, he set about learning all he could about the person he wanted to destroy.

On his new burner phone, he called a buddy who could help him trace license plates. Once he found out the owner's name, he Googled it, trying to determine the connection, if any, to Penny Wells. After about three hours of concentrated searching, he had three names he felt might be a connection to Penny. He also now knew the name of the man who visited Hilltop regularly. He was a lawyer. "That might be helpful. Maybe I could find some connection on that Ancestry site. It sure would be trick getting close to the family without them knowing." Tennent smiled as he sat back in his chair. "I'll get that snot-faced bitch somehow, even if it's the last thing I do. I want her dead. It's worth spending the rest of my life in the big house if I can eliminate her stinkin' existence from this earth." His voice spoke with an evil vengeance to a non-existent audience.

"Deke," he shouted when his cell phone rang. "Just the man I need. Gotta talk to ya. Meet me at that beer joint, Hair of the Dog."

"Sure, Bill, when?"

"For lunch today if you can manage it."

"Track is closed today. I got nothin' but time on my hands. Meet you in about an hour."

"Hey, buddy." Bill was all smiles as Deke sat down and joined him in the corner booth.

"Yer awful cheerful, considering."

"Considering what, Deke?"

"Yer brain is going round and round. I can see it."

"I need your help."

"I ain't doin' nuthin' that ain't legal." Deke began to rise and leave.

"This is all very legit. I'm paying you to help me." Tennent believed offering Deke money would ensure he would not have to do all the legwork he was planning.

"All I want you to do is follow three different cars for a week each and see if they go to that cunt's house. Follow and get the low down on anyone connected with her. Write down the addresses, take pictures of the houses and the person driving the car. Your cell phone does take pictures, doesn't it?"

"Yes, boss."

"In the meantime, I'm going to look up and see if I have any family history connection to the name Worley. Ancestry.com, here I come."

"Why are you doing that?"

"I want to find another entrée into the Wells family contingent. Maybe I can find a relative I'm connected with. Bring me back a report as soon as you can."

Tennent spent many waking hours on the computer searching the DNA website. "Well, lookie here, wadda ya know. My great-grandmother's sister was married to a Worley. That's not too common a name. Well, great-aunt

Alice, how nice to meet you here. No time like the present to meet a prospective nephew."

A malevolent look appeared on Tennent's face as he grabbed a piece of fine vellum paper and wrote a brief message.

8

The secretary brought a short handwritten letter to Tom's
office. He sat back in his leather chair as he read the note.
"I never had a great-aunt Alice. I wonder if this is true."
Tom placed a call to his mother.

"Mom, did Gramma ever have a sister named
Alice?"

His mother became strangely quiet. "Well, I had an
Aunt Alice by marriage. She would have been your great-
great-aunt. She was married at one time to my great-
grandfather's uncle. You never met him. Everyone in the
family counseled her not to marry him, but she did
anyway. When she died, the coroner called it a suicide,
but we believe your great-great-uncle had something to do
with it. He died in prison for an unrelated crime. This is a
subject your father and I consider closed. Don't open
Pandora's box, Tom. It could be dangerous."

"Now, you have me intrigued. I received a letter
this morning from a Bill Tennent telling me he thinks he is

my uncle, or maybe even a cousin. He'd like to come to my office and meet me."

"Oh, Tom, I'm not sure that is so wise. Be careful."

"Of course, I will, Mother. I have to go to a meeting. Love you."

Tom waited almost two weeks before he made the phone call. "Mr. Tennent, this is Thomas Worley."

"Oh, Tom, Please, call me Uncle Bill. I would so love to meet you. I've been out of the country for too many years."

"Sir, I don't believe you are related to me. I never had an Aunt Alice. Wherever you obtained your information, it's not correct."

"But I saw the information on Ancestry. Isn't their work supposed to supply an accurate listing?" Tennent was gritting his teeth, on the verge of losing his cool. He had to grab the arm of the chair he was sitting in to keep from yelling into the phone.

"For the most part, I would imagine so." Tom wanted to get off the phone, sensing irritation with the caller. "Mr. Tennent, I am late for a meeting and must end this conversation. I wish you luck in finding your relative. Goodbye, sir."

Tennent sat back in his chair; he had yet to put the cell phone back down on the table. Deflated from the conversation, he began talking to himself. *Well, at least I have Deke working on the car angle. There's more than one way to skin a cat.*

9

Lynn invited Tom to Hilltop. It happened to be the same
day Vinnie, Michel, Jean-Luc, and Penny descended on
Trudy to surprise her on her birthday. Ursula had prepared
a special dinner and a masterpiece of a cake for dessert.
The conversation was fast and furious between them.
Penny mentioned she hired a bodyguard.

This was something new to Tom, and he wanted to
know more about the added security.

"Ever since I had the painting stolen, even before
that, I have been hounded by this man. He is a relentless,
ill-tempered scoundrel. First, he tried to destroy my
reputation, almost with success, and then, he tried to steal
another priceless Driscoll painting from my gallery. But
we caught him, well the authorities did. He spent several
years in prison for that crime. He was recently released,
and we believe he is following me, using a disguise. He is
a master at changing his looks and identity."

"That's terrible, Penny. What's his name? If you

want to tell me."

"Tennent, Bill Tennent." Penny scoffed.

Tom gulped. "He called me on the phone! Told me I was his long-lost nephew, and I should call him Uncle Bill."

"Is that true, Tom? Is he your uncle?" Lynn withdrew her hand he had been holding.

"Well, it could be. I don't know. My mother tells me her grandmother had an Aunt Alice, but she left the family and married a man, of which none approved. Her husband ended up dying in prison. We have no idea what happened to her. The maiden name was Worley. Tennent said his Aunt Alice was a Worley. He got all the information online at Ancestry. I told him I had no Aunt Alice and there was a gross error. Then I said I had a meeting and had to hang up. Oh, Penny, I hope this won't cause you any problem."

Jean-Luc piped up. "Well, at least I think you have cut off an avenue for him to get closer to the family. It also tells us he somehow found out Tom was visiting here, who he was and wanted to make inroads."

"What a bastard." Trudy was quick to add. "He's caused nothing but misery for Penny and Vinnie when she was younger. We had that letter from the Department of Corrections telling us he was being released. His contempt must have festered while he was in prison."

"Some people never give up until they have taken full revenge," Michel said.

"Now that we are all here, we should make some flight plans." Trudy got down to business. "Since Tennent is obviously around and doing whatever he can to find out about Penny, we need to keep her out of the limelight. I think it is best to stick together and travel on the same flight, safety in numbers. I think we should all stay in the same hotel. I can make flight reservations if you want me to. I'll ask the travel agent to take care of hotel and car rental accommodations."

"Trudy, I would like to travel with Tom if he can manage the time." Lynn gave her a sweet smile.

Penny spoke up. "I could travel on the same flight also. Jean-Luc, do you want to come with us?"

"Perfect, Penny. I am going to see if Adrian can join us in Berlin."

"Trudy, how can we find out who has been managing Ernst's property all these years?"

"I think that should be the job for Tom. He's the

lawyer, and lawyers must have access to lawyers in other countries. Am I right, Tom?"

"My firm could send out an email blast to see if we receive any answers."

"That might be the quickest way to do it." Jean-Luc nodded his approval.

"If we receive confirmation from an agency in Berlin, my firm could partner with them on everything. If they are good, it could save the estate considerable money."

"Speaking of money," Penny interrupted, "Trudy, do you think Ernst could have left any money in Berlin?"

"I have no idea. When Ernst left Berlin, he hid as much currency as he could carry on his person, but he must have left some funds behind to cover expenses. I think we should speak with the bankers who handled his money here. They must be more equipped than we are to find out. Tom, if you would like me to, I can take care of that detail. If the bank can't or won't answer my inquiries, I'll turn the matter over to you," Trudy volunteered.

"All right. I will book the plane and hotel reservations for Penny and Lynn, Tom and Jean-Luc. Is that okay with everyone? And Lynn, I promise I will come with Vinnie and Michel once I wrap up my business in Texas. You certainly will be surrounded by your friends."

"I love it, Trudy." Lynn embraced Trudy and kissed her cheek.

The following day, Trudy called her friend at a local travel agency, booked all the tickets and rooms for everyone. Then she asked her to courier the entire package to her, but not with a regular courier. "I will send my own courier to pick up and deliver the package."

"Why?" Her travel agency friend found the request unusual.

"Nothing illegal is going on, trust me. Recently we've had some problems in the family, and I don't want to exacerbate it. Call me when you have all the details worked out, and a courier from the police department will stop by to pick up the package."

10

"I doubt if anyone will recognize me." Tennent combed his mustache and studied his appearance. "Dark glasses will complete my wardrobe. Now I will take a trip to the museum and see if I can find the bitch." He then began his daily ritual of visiting the museum to see if he could spot the red-headed woman he loathed with a passion. It took almost a month, but one day his patience finally paid off as he stood in one of the gallery rooms and overheard a conversation. Tennent turned slightly and saw her. His pulse raced with fury as he watched her walk away. "I'll follow you now. You won't be able to strut your hoity-toity shit around anymore."

He sat in a nondescript car in the employee parking lot. Through his binoculars, he watched the museum employees leave. Shortly before six, Tennent was rewarded with seeing Penny go. He watched her climb into a white BMW 350. She left the parking lot with Tennent in tow a few car lengths behind. The felon followed her until she drove through a locked gate at the condominium project.

"Expensive digs."

Tennent began a new daily ritual of following Penny after work. One day he realized she was leading him to a house in Laguna. "Damn, I can't go through the gates to the top of the hill. I wonder if she still has the gallery. Only one way to find out."

11

Trudy greeted a fashionably dressed man standing in the middle of the gallery admiring the new acquisitions.

"Good morning. Welcome to the Galerie L'Heritage. Please make yourself comfortable. May I bring you a cup of coffee?"

"That would be very nice," said the disguised man as he smiled at her. "The paintings are superb. What is that one in the security box? It's beautiful." Tennent laid on all the charm he could muster.

"It is magnificent and isn't for sale. It's a Driscoll from a private collection."

"You're certain the owner won't part with it?"

"I'm quite certain. This particular one, Sunset over Tuscany, hung in her parent's home. After they died, it was bequeathed to the Smithsonian. It just hasn't been sent there yet."

"I'm so sorry, my deepest condolences to whomever the painting belongs." Tennent could have been playing harp strings. He was filled with sincerity.

"How very kind of you. I will relay your thoughts to Ms. Wells. Is there another painting that might be of interest?" Trudy thought he must have money to spend.

"Let me look around for a bit. If I see something, I'll let you know."

"Thank you, Mr…oh, you never did say your name."

"It's Smith, Bill Smith."

"I'm Trudy King, gallery manager and long-time friend of Ms. Wells."

"A pleasure to meet you. I must say this has been a lovely morning. Rest assured. I'll be back."

"I'll be looking forward to seeing you."

Trudy couldn't wait to tell Penny about the charming man that came to the gallery. "He oozed charm and sophistication, Penny. His clothes were Savile Row. He had a mustache and a graying goatee. I couldn't see his eyes because he wore dark glasses. Come to think of it, how strange he never took them off."

Penny's thoughts were whirling. "Trudy, a man like you have described has been haunting my workplace. Every time I go out on the museum floor, he's there. Do you think?"

"Do you think it could be Tennent in disguise?"
Trudy waited for Penny's reply.

"He looks about 65 or 70. I'm going to call Jean-Luc.
I think I needed that bodyguard before we even talked about
it at Vinnie and Michel's."

Tennent had Deke driving all over Los Angeles and Orange
County, running fool's errands.

"Okay, we know that white BMW belongs to the
bitch. Lavinia and her husband own the Cadillac. He's the
doc that sewed me up in New York many years ago. The
other car, that older model Ford belongs to the young lawyer,
Thomas Worley. I can't believe we are not related.
Something doesn't feel right." Tennent was agitated, plotting
his next move.

"What more do you need me to do, boss? I'm getting
tired of driving all over creation. I wonder if they spotted my
tail." Deke had collapsed in Tennent's only comfortable
chair, but not before he pulled a beer out of the fridge.

12

The following Saturday evening, Trudy hosted a small dinner party and invited Penny, Lavinia, Michel, Jean-Luc, and Lynn. Tom Worley was also invited, much to the delight of the young violinist.

Ursula was passing a bountiful tray of crab and shrimp canapés around the room.

Tom clinked glasses with Lynn as he held a glass of white Sauvignon Blanc in one hand and a crab cake in the other.

"Did you say your concert is next Saturday night? I'd love to attend."

"I can get you a seat, but you may have to sit in the press box unless someone turns in a ticket."

"I don't care where I sit. I just want to be able to hear you perform."

"Tom," Penny spoke up. "All of us will be meeting at a restaurant near Segerstrom for dinner if you would like to join us. Lynn, of course, will be backstage and not joining us until the concert is over. We will then go over to Harbor Isle to Lavinia's and Michel's home for some celebratory champagne."

"Sounds wonderful. Thank you for including me." He smiled at Lynn. *I never thought a letter from a deceased client would introduce me to such a beautiful soul. My feelings for her are growing fast and strong.*

13

A few weeks after the Segerstrom concert, the conductor called Lynn. "Aisalynn, how are you?" His voice boomed over the phone.

"Fine, I'm practicing and practicing. How are you, Maestro?"

"In good health. The reason for my call is that I will be conducting a concert at Davies Hall while Tilson Thomas is on vacation. My soloist just came down with pneumonia, and at his advanced age, I don't want to take any chances of his collapsing on stage because he hasn't fully recovered."

"That would be terrible for him and you." Lynn was solicitous in her reply.

"Indeed. I would like you to play in his place."

Lynn was speechless. "I would be honored. When is the concert? What would I be playing?" Lynn could not contain her excitement.

"Tchaikovsky, the D Major. You would have three

weeks to practice. One week in San Francisco for rehearsal and then the performance that Saturday night."

"My answer is yes, yes, and yes! I cannot thank you enough, Maestro. You have put so much faith in me. I will not let you down."

"You are a talented artist, Aisalynn. I know it's short notice, but you can do it. If I can give you another showcase, it would be my pleasure. I will have my secretary call you in a few days with all the arrangements, your compensation, and so forth."

"I'll be waiting for her call." Lynn, bursting with joy, was bouncing on cloud nine. "I'll see you in a few weeks, Maestro. Thank you again so very much. Goodbye."

Lynn hung up the phone and began screaming in delight, bringing Trudy and Ursula running.

"What's wrong?" The two of them said in chorus.

"Nothing! Only the most exciting news! I've been invited to play in Davies Hall, San Francisco, in one month."

"That is an incredible opportunity, Lynn, but we will have to reschedule your departure to Berlin by a week or so. I don't think it will be a problem. I'll contact the travel agent so arrangements can be changed."

"Trudy, you're wonderful. I'm going to call Camilla now and tell her my good news. I must have the entire concerto memorized before I go to San Francisco. That only gives me three weeks. I've played it many times before, but not as the soloist."

"I worry about you being alone in San Francisco for ten days. Are you sure you wouldn't like me to join you?"

"Maybe for the last few days and, of course, for the performance. They keep an apartment at Opera Plaza for guest artists, that is where I will be staying. It's only a one-block walk to Davies. The secretary told me there is a popular restaurant on the main floor. They serve breakfast, lunch, and dinner, and if I don't want to eat out, there's a grocery store and a pharmacy on the premises. I'll be just fine, Trudy."

"I'm only worried because of that demented Bill Tennent. That man has a screw loose, and I don't want him coming after you to get to Penny."

"Will you take me to the airport?"

"Of course, I will. Orange County has several airlines that fly directly to San Francisco. I'll book your ticket. Take a taxi to Opera Plaza, not a bus. After your practice session today, we are going shopping for a gown for you. This is a momentous occasion, and you deserve a new dress. I am thinking of something long and flowing. Something very understated with great lines. And don't worry about the price. It's my gift to you."

"Trudy, you are extra special." Lynn put her arms around the older woman in a warm embrace and smothered her with kisses. She bounced on the balls of her feet with excitement.

"Let me breathe," Trudy giggled. "Two new dress shops have opened in town, both advertising evening gowns as their specialty. If we can't find anything at either of those boutiques, we will head for Nordys."

"I'm off to find my Tchaikovsky score now and practice, practice and practice. I'll be in the living room. You can interrupt me around 3:30. Thank you for everything. You're wonderful, Trudy. I hope you know that."

14

"Camilla, I've been invited to play in Davies Hall. I'm beyond the moon with excitement. Will you give me some extra coaching sessions, maybe two a week?"

After Lynn hung up the phone, she put the concerto on her music stand, used the resin on her bowstrings, and began to play the first movement. Realizing how difficult it would be with all the pizzicato on the strings, she asked Trudy to find her a record or tape of the concerto. *I need some instruction from a master. Itzak Perlman will be perfect.*

For the next several days, Lynn woke listening to the concerto and going to bed in the evening with the concerto playing on her tape recorder. *I'll get you mastered, my friend.*

The three weeks passed faster than Lynn wanted, but Camilla was happy with the results. "You will do a wonderful job on the concerto. Just remember, even with all the right notes, let your audience feel your emotion through your playing. A technical performance is not a good thing. Aisalynn, I think the Maestro will be pleased with your performance. I am."

On the day the violinist was packing for her trip, Trudy thought it would be prudent for her to bring the concert dress with her so Lynn would not have to worry about it.

"That's a great idea, Trudy. Now all I have to worry about is work clothes and some cosmetics. I'm not going to do anything different with my hair than I did at the Segerstrom so that I won't need a hair appointment. No flashy jewelry, just a pair of earrings, and I might wear a post rather than anything dangling."

"I think that is a smart solution."

Trudy took Lynn to the Orange County airport the next morning, and by one o'clock, Lynn called to let her know she had arrived safely and would be on her way to the concert hall for rehearsal. When practice concluded for the evening, some of the orchestra's younger members wanted to go out for a drink. Lynn excused herself for being overly tired, stopped by the Plaza restaurant, ordered a sandwich to go, and retired to her apartment. The call for rehearsal was at 10 am. Lynn didn't even finish her food before she was sound asleep.

The rehearsals went as planned, and the Maestro seemed pleased with her interpretation of the concerto. Lynn continued a daily routine of at least one hour of practice, not including the hall's daily rehearsal. Saturday night would be her big moment, and she wanted it perfect.

15

One of Tennent's ex-con cohorts reported seeing Trudy driving Lynn to the airport. She had a violin case and one carry-on bag.

"Thanks for the info, man. She must be going to play another concert, not far away if not much luggage."

Tennent found a newsstand and looked at Las Vegas, Salt Lake City, Portland, and San Francisco papers. Once he turned to the music page of the *Chronicle*, he found what he was looking for: Aisalynn Sheperd would be performing with the San Francisco Symphony on Saturday evening. He knew her friends would be in attendance, so he went ahead and secured himself a ticket for the concert. *They would never suspect me of going to San Fran to attack them!*

The audience and the Maestro warmly received Lynn as she made her way to the center stage. She felt regal in the dress Trudy had purchased for her, shimmering ice-blue satin with only tailoring to showcase the stitching and cut's elegance. The gown was off her shoulders with cap sleeves, the skirt, mermaid style yet wide enough to provide ease of movement. Lynn had combed her shiny black hair into a sophisticated-looking French twist. At least that is what the newspaper would say when reviewing the concert.

Observing the Maestro, she put her violin under her chin and poised the bow, ready to begin. Even though a lengthy concerto, time flew by onstage. She knew she had given a superb performance.

Tom stood in the wings with an abundant bouquet of red roses. "You were wonderful!"

"I'm so glad you're here. Not everyone can come backstage."

"Before you change out of your gown, your admirers from Southern California would like you to see them outside the stage door where we can take pictures with this beautiful artist."

A dirty and disheveled homeless man stood under a lamppost watching all the photographs being taken.

16

Penny and Lynn were standing together, waiting for the next photograph to be taken, all laughs and smiles. An arm with a long blade flashed across Lynn's neck. Everyone stood stunned as the assailant fled into the night.

Jean-Luc screamed, "Call 911!" He took out his large white handkerchief and held it tightly on the blood streaming from Lynn's neck. "I know this is Tennent's calling card. Lynn, we are going to have to get you a bodyguard too. You're a fortunate young lady. If that knife had been a millimeter deeper into your neck, we would be calling a coroner."

Lynn, traumatized by the violence, stood comatose. Shock was setting in by the time the police and ambulance arrived. Tom accompanied her to the nearest hospital. Oblivious to her surroundings, every question she answered was monosyllable, yes, no.

Trudy and Penny gathered her belongings from the dressing room and the apartment while Jean-Luc went to find the Maestro to inform him of the attack.

"I'm horrified. Such violence does not happen around here. How is she? Will Aisalynn be able to perform in the future?"

"I'm certain she will. It will take her time to heal. We have a trip planned to Berlin in a few weeks. I know the change of scenery and a new adventure will be good for her."

The Maestro handed Jean-Luc his business card. "Please do keep me informed. I want to know how Aisalynn is healing. She has a brilliant career ahead of her."

Lynn, stunned by the late-night knifing, snuggled next to Tom on the plane trip home. Trudy, Penny, and Jean-Luc sat nearby. The five of them were the only passengers in first class.

"Do you think you can handle a plane trip to Berlin, Lynn? It's a long flight. Maybe you would like to stay over in New York and rest for a few days." Penny was overly concerned about her well-being.

"Penny, I would love to stop in New York, but we need to make the most of your time before you return to work. I know I'll be okay if we are flying first class."

"Yes, you are." Trudy popped up from the magazine she was perusing. "Under the circumstances of what you've been through, I wouldn't let you fly any other way."

"Then it's settled. We will be leaving a week from Sunday. Trudy, is it possible to hire a limo for all of us? We can begin in Laguna Beach with Jean-Luc and me and stop in Pasadena for Penny and Tom."

"That's a wonderful idea, Lynn. You know I haven't returned to Berlin since I took Ursula to her relatives in New York. She stayed with them until I had a house where she could live."

"Trudy, that's incredible. You came to see me at the Driscoll right after that. You and I planned to move to California. Someday, we will all have to get together, you, Vinnie, and even Vie Lee, and write our story. I'm not sure people would believe it."

"You know Penny, truth is stranger than fiction."

The pilot's voice came through the loudspeaker. "Ladies and gentlemen, please fasten your seat belts and put your seat in the upright position. We will be landing shortly."

"Who has a car at the airport?" They were landing at Orange County. Jean-Luc looked at the ladies and Tom.

"I think you are the only one, Jean-Luc. Tom flew out of Burbank, and so did Penny. I took Lynn, and you came on your own. I worry about getting Lynn home safely. Tom and Penny can work out their plan between them. Your car only holds two, so you're no help." An overly tired Trudy laughed at her own joke.

Unable to find a limo at the airport, she engaged a taxi to ride back to Hilltop. When Trudy finally turned off her bedside lamp, she sunk exhausted onto her soft pillows.

It was only because the phone rang, she awakened. When she looked at her bedside clock, it said 2:00. *I couldn't have slept that long.*

"Mrs. King, this is Camilla Wickes. In the paper this morning, I read that an artist was slashed after the performance at Davies Hall. That's not our dear Aisalynn, is it?"

"Yes, unfortunately, it was. It happened so fast. We are so grateful the knife wound didn't cause any permanent damage."

"I'm so glad." The paper said it was a homeless man. I hope they catch him."

"So do I. You will be pleased to know the Maestro has taken Aisalynn under his wing, so to speak, and he can't wait until she is ready to perform under his baton again."

"Aisalynn has a great career in her future. She is a magnificent violinist at her young age. You may tell Aisalynn I called and asked about her. And congratulations on what the newspapers called an 'outstanding performance.' I will talk with her later. Goodbye."

Trudy made a phone call to Lynn's doctor for a prescription for her to use while traveling. Next, a phone call to Jean-Luc, asking him to pick up the medicine for her as she had so much to do to see Lynn packed and ready for Berlin.

"Jean-Luc, it has been so many years since I set foot in Berlin, I don't even begin to know what kind of clothes she should bring."

"I think all she is going to need are jeans, sweatpants, and shirts. She may want a jacket or sweater. Maybe a nice pair of slacks and a blouse in case we do something special. We are not going on a pleasure trip, although we will be dining out every night, I believe."

"I know. I want her to have everything she might need. She is going to want to take her violin, music, and stand so she can practice."

"We will love listening to her as we catalog whatever there is to catalog. Changing the subject, two questions for you. One, did Tom manage to locate the firm that oversaw the property for Ernst, and two, was Lynn's gown salvageable from the blood on it?"

"Tom did manage to find the firm, and one of their staff will meet you at the airport. The dress is still at the cleaners. I do hope they can clean it. After all, it is an original design and is special to Lynn. Do you know if the limo is picking you up first, or will it be Lynn?"

"I asked that I be picked up first. Good lord, today is Thursday, and we are leaving early Sunday morning. I haven't even thought about packing either. I'll be up to see you two tomorrow. Am I invited for dinner?"

"As always, Jean-Luc, there is always a seat at our table for you. See you then."

Dinner with Trudy was usually a lively affair, but everyone was quiet, conversation subdued. Ursula walked into the dining room. "Trudy, I have something important to discuss with you."

"Ursula, please come and join us while we indulge in one of your glorious desserts. What is on your mind?"

"Trudy, I've known you since you were a little girl. Now you're beyond retirement age, so you know where that puts me. I want to retire. Jean-Luc, the building where your father lived has a lovely front apartment perfectly suited for my needs. I told the superintendent I would take it. I've already put down a deposit."

"Ursula, what will we do without you? What will I do without you? I have no idea what you'll be paying for your apartment, but you will never have to worry about the rent. I'll take care of it. Your social security should be able to cover the rest of your expenses. If not, I will supplement."

"Trudy, I didn't mean for you to do that." Tears were coming down on Ursula's cheeks, even though she was smiling. "I can't thank you enough for all you have done for me."

"You are part of all our families. Not just mine. Please don't be scarce with your visits. When are you planning to make the move?"

"I thought while you were in Berlin, I would begin moving my things. I certainly would not leave the house unattended while you're gone."

"It will seem so strange not having you here. Tell me about your apartment."

"Well, as you know, I don't drive, so I had to find a place convenient for shopping. There's a grocery store down the block, and I'm only a block and a half from the beach."

"Sounds just lovely, Ursula."

Lynn made one of her few comments of the evening. "May I come over and have some more cooking lessons?"

"You know you are always welcome, my child."

"Tom loves all your Italian flavors. And I want to learn to make that famous strudel of yours."

"Are we seeing a wedding in the future? If so, it would be my pleasure to cater it, as long as you aren't inviting the world." The lighthearted remark eased the tension and everyone laughed.

"Well, he hasn't proposed yet."

"He will," said Trudy.

"I second that," Jean-Luc added.

When the limo arrived on Sunday morning, Trudy stood in the driveway with Lynn and her luggage. Jean-Luc stepped out from the back seat and walked toward Trudy. She put her arms on his shoulders so that he would look directly at her.

"I'm counting on you, Jean-Luc. Once you're in the air, don't forget to give Lynn one of those pills from the bottle you picked up at the pharmacy for me. Lynn's doctor said she should sleep for at least eight hours. She needs rest and plenty of it. I don't know if the first class section has beds, but if she can sleep for most of the flight, Lynn should be fine by the time you land in Berlin."

"You take care of yourself, Trudy." Lynn put her arms around her. "I'll be waiting to see you in Berlin. I love you."

Trudy teared up. "Lynn, you take care of yourself, don't overdo. Let Tom do the legwork if there is any."

"Yes, Trudy. I promise I'll be good." She kissed her on the cheek.

"Have a great and safe flight. I'll see you in two weeks."

Trudy continued to wave as the limo went down the hill and out of sight.

17

Trudy didn't know where to focus her eyes first as she walked out of the airport. She could not believe all the changes. *It's absolutely beautiful and modern. I'm amazed.*

"Lynn, Tom. It's wonderful to see you both." She hugged them tightly. "Lynn, you look healthy, radiant."

"I guess I'm the culprit," said Tom as he hugged Lynn. "I adore you, Aisalynn Sheperd. Let's take Trudy over to the house."

Trudy looked for her old house on the way, but it had been torn down; a skyscraper stood in its place. As they passed Checkpoint Charlie, she looked up and saw the watchtower, reminding her of how impenetrable the iron curtain had been. The transformation left Trudy momentarily tongue-tied, saying nothing but 'ooh' and 'aah.'

"All these lovely outdoor restaurants, the bright umbrellas, the myriad of flowers. It's beautiful." She turned to Lynn. "Honey, you should have no problem receiving top dollar for your property."

"According to the people I've spoken with, Lynn should be able to net a minimum of ten million after the sale. My firm recommended a good tax attorney here so we can figure out how to maximize her money with the least amount of taxes."

"What about the house? What kind of shape is it in?" Trudy had many questions.

"Wait till you see it and talk with Jean-Luc and Adrian. If we work hard, we all should be able to leave Germany in the two weeks you've allotted to stay here. Would you like to drop off your suitcases at the hotel?"

"Please, Tom, that would be wonderful. I must take pictures so I can send them to Ursula. She won't believe the changes. She is excited to move into her new apartment while we are here in Berlin."

"She has always been a hard worker and deserves some happiness," Lynn added to the conversation.

Once the porter had taken Trudy's luggage from the car, Tom drove them to Ernst's house.

"It looks better than I remembered it."

"Wait till you see the inside," Lynn boasted.

Trudy's eyes scanned from wall to wall as she admired the paintings. "Unreal. Ernst left behind a fortune in art to come to America." She walked into another room and saw Jean-Luc and Adrian studying another painting. "Hey, you two." She greeted them both with a hug. Adrian, in his French manner, kissed her on both cheeks.

"Bonjour, Trudy. It is wonderful to see you."

"You too, Adrian. Where's Penny?"

"Busy cataloging all our finds, putting them in some semblance of order. She wants all of them shipped to the Los Angeles County Museum of Art. She believes this might be the art show of the decade."

"Penny, it's so good to see you." Trudy gave her friend a warm hug and a kiss on her left cheek. "I'm sorry Vinnie and Michel couldn't make the trip. But I'm thrilled to be here. After all these many years, I can't believe how remarkable this old house looks. I remember the last time you and I were here. Scary, the iron curtain, the soldiers. I shudder when I think that the guards might have asked you questions."

"Good lord, Trudy, I try to forget that day. So much has happened since then. I can't believe all the magnificent artwork Ernst has collected. Once I'm through cataloging all the paintings and art objects, Jean-Luc and Adrian will see they are packed and shipped."

"How many do you have?"

"Would you believe over one hundred? I don't think the museum would showcase all of them, but certainly the majority. The rest, Lynn can sell, keep for her private collection or donate to another museum. She's already found one she won't part with; it's a picture of a female violinist."

"Do you think it might be the woman whose violin may still be here?"

"Unknown, but the painting certainly spoke to her. Let's take a break and have a cup of tea, or would you rather have a glass of wine? It's just about that time of the afternoon."

"Yes, wine, please. That sounds very refreshing."

"The boys went wine tasting and brought back several vintages for us to sample. I think it would be fun for all of us to be out on the patio so we can visit."

Lynn and Tom were missing when the glasses were poured. "Two people in love are probably somewhere on the grounds."

18

Tom held Lynn's hand as they strolled through the back garden. Filled with flowering plants and shade trees, it reminded Lynn of pictures she had seen in magazines describing opulent gardens of the world. The two sat on a stone bench beneath an arbor of roses and breathed in the fragrant blooms. Tom fidgeted in his pocket for a moment, pulled out a small box, knelt, and presented the box to Lynn.

"I love you more than anything in the world, Lynn. Would you do me the honor of becoming my wife?"

Lynn beamed as her eyes filled with tears of happiness. "Yes! Oh yes, Tom. I love you so much. This ring looks antique, and the diamond is magnificent."

"The ring belonged to my grandmother."

"I'm honored to wear it."

The two embraced the loving moment. "I know Trudy will be so pleased. She told me the day you first came to the house that you were a keeper. I think I fell in love with you that day too."

"Let's go tell everyone. I want to tell the world." Tom held her tightly, his arm around her narrow waist. Together they walked to the patio, giddy with happiness.

"Who swallowed the canary?" Jean-Luc laughed as he said it.

"We have something to tell you." Lynn and Tom said at the same moment.

"You don't even need to tell us. We can tell by your faces. When is the wedding?" Jean-Luc stood up, shook hands with the groom, and kissed the bride-to-be.

"We have no idea yet. I want a small wedding, maybe at Hilltop if that's okay with Trudy. Ursula has already told me her gift would be the catering."

"I'd love to have it there, Lynn," said Trudy.

Penny turned the conversation to a serious tone. "First things first, however. I need to see all these paintings packed, crated, and shipped to the museum for me to curate. Second, we need to decide which artifacts should go where. I may want some for the museum. Trudy, do you want a painting or two for the gallery?"

"Of course, I would love that."

"When the house is empty," said Trudy, "we need to get x-ray equipment to check the walls and floors. We don't want to miss any space where Ernst could have hidden something, especially search for that violin Ursula said was here."

Tom broke into the conversation. "Adrian, do you know anyone who might have that type of equipment in Europe. I know someone back home, but it would be more feasible to find someone here.'

"I will ask around. Sure saves the estate a bit of money if we can find someone locally."

"I also talked with the lawyers here, and they have recommended two different real estate companies," said Tom.

"I'm wondering if we can't just go to the hotel companies directly and ask if they're interested in purchasing the property," Adrian asked Tom.

"We probably could, but I think it would be more prudent to use a real estate person, and if they pay a referral fee to the law firm, that would be an added bonus for us to give them." Tom was definite in his response.

"Good thinking there," Penny said.

Trudy pulled out her cell phone. "Now I think it would be a good idea to call a taxi. We can go to one of those cafes on Frederichstrasse and have a festive celebration dinner for Lynn and Tom's engagement."

Dinner was a lively affair. Trudy spoke in German to diners at the surrounding tables about what she and her party were celebrating. Toast upon toast was offered, with best wishes for a long and prosperous marriage. By the time they returned to their hotel for the night, it was early in the morning.

"Sleep, that's all I want right now," Lynn said, yawning at everyone. "That was some party," she said to herself when she awakened in the early afternoon.

Jean-Luc found Penny looking over another set of paintings. "Penny, do you want these shipped by container or sent by plane?"

"I'd love to do it by container, but I think it would be faster if they were all shipped together by plane. Maybe we could fly with the cargo?"

"Adrian has a friend who flies a large corporate jet. Maybe we could prevail on him during his downtime."

"That would be fantastic. Ask, please."

Adrian was able to supply a favorable answer. "If we can have everything ready within five days, Claude can do it. He will fly into a private airport near Berlin. We should have everything ready to go at the airport when we're told, and he will take the lot to Los Angeles. There would be room for Jean-Luc and me to travel with the cargo, but the rest of you would have to fly commercial."

19

Packers arrived the next day. Everyone was glad Trudy was there to give instructions in German. "It's been so long since I've spoken German. The words aren't coming that easily," she told Penny.

"Yes, but they understand you better than my having to use my hands to demonstrate everything," Penny told Trudy. "See how carefully they must pack the frames. Heaven forbid anything is broken or scratched en route."

Penny labeled and numbered each painting with a corresponding description on the papers she had been cataloging. It was a tedious and painstaking job but could only be done by one person, leaving the others unable to assist in the process.

Trudy walked through the rooms and looked at all the antique furniture. "It's all beautiful," she commented, "but much too heavy to move. Lynn, when you have a moment, could you come to the dining room, please," she called out.

Lynn could be heard practicing. "I'll be right there."

"Lynn, don't let me influence you, but," said Trudy, "all this furniture is much too heavy to transport to the United States. There is a high demand for period-pieces such as this. I don't know how much you would get for it, but a boutique hotel might like to buy it. It's very expensive German-made furniture, Biedermeier, and the condition is exceptional, considering its age."

"I have no attachment to it. I think that is a great idea, Trudy. Tom and I are meeting with a real estate broker this afternoon. We're going to his office, not here. I don't want anyone on the premises until we decide which broker we're going to use."

"That's very smart."

"It was Tom's idea, and I agree with him. He thinks we should be discreet and have everything out of the house that we plan to take with us. We don't want a broker asking to keep this or that for potential buyers."

The packers worked from morning until the sun set and still had not finished. "We'll be back tomorrow morning. I'm sure we can finish by the afternoon," the lead packer informed Trudy.

Overjoyed when she heard his remarks, Trudy relayed the news to Penny.

"Wonderful. Is there something here you might want to take in remembrance of Ernst?"

"I sort of liked that gaudy crystal peacock with the blue crystal feathers. I think it might be a fun thing to keep at the gallery. It certainly would spark conversation. Someday in the future, if you decide to close the gallery, the peacock can grace the table in the sunroom at Hilltop. His feathers will really sparkle the sunlight."

"How true. You could take it in your suitcase or carry it in your purse. It's big enough to hold the piece.'

"No digs at the size of my purse, please."

"Just commenting, my friend." They both laughed.

"Big purses come in handy when I'm traveling. Take this crystal peacock, for example. He will be very cozy in the large inner side pocket."

Penny stretched and performed a couple of standing yoga moves. "It's wine time. I'm ready for a big glass. I've been marking and counting and describing right along with the packers."

"I know. You've been doing a yeoman's job."

20

While Tom and Lynn were meeting the real estate broker, the four friends sat at the garden patio table and polished off a crisp, chilled bottle of Kabinett Reisling. "This is better than I remembered," said Trudy as she held her glass out for a second round. "I heard about this great fish restaurant. Would you like to try it for dinner?"

Tom was able to secure the services of a man who had an x-ray machine designed explicitly for looking through solid surfaces. The device is used to search demolition sites before the structures are felled. Although he spoke no English, Trudy conveyed that they wanted all the walls and floors searched. "Ernst helped so many Jews before he fled to the states. We can never be certain of all that might be hidden."

"How long will it take you to search the house?"

"About a day and a half." The astute gentleman estimated. "It will take longer if we have to break into the walls to retrieve objects."

"Just be very thorough, as I know you will." Trudy led him to the area where she wanted him to begin his search. Nothing was discovered after the first three rooms were examined.

"Tom, don't forget this place has a basement. As far as I can recall, it is not large, so it shouldn't take long to examine the walls. I doubt anything would be put under the concrete floor. Repairing the floor would have been far too difficult. The walls would be the best place to hide anything. I can't manage the stairs with my arthritis, but maybe you could go down there."

Tom motioned to the man and his machine to follow him to the dining room. "The basement is concealed beneath the rug." The two men pulled the carpet back and gingerly descended the stairs.

"Ach de Lieber," came a cry from the man and the machine. "Look what I've found."

"A cache of silver. Look at this antique. It is a samovar with a matching serving tray." Tom announced as he brought the discovery upstairs.

Trudy called Penny and Lynn to join them in the dining room. "This is Yemenite silver, and look here…there is a name engraved on the platter, Rubinstein. How fascinating. Penny, these pieces must go into the exhibit."

"I can put it on display. And when it's over, Lynn, there is no doubt you could sell it. This silver is in pristine condition; it just needs a deep polishing to restore its luster. You'd get top dollar for each piece."

"I'd be glad to do that. Make sure you separate my painting of the violinist. I want to take it back to Laguna and can pick it up at the museum, airport, or wherever is most convenient for you."

Penny cataloged twenty pieces of various types of matching silver and had the packers put them in a separate box to go along with the paintings.

"We still haven't found the violin if it's here," said Trudy.

"I'll go back in the basement and check the other wall," the x-ray man told Trudy in German.

"Danke."

A long half-hour passed when another whoop and holler came from the basement. The man came up triumphantly holding a dusty violin case.

"Lynn! Lynn!" Everyone was excited for her to come to the dining room. Her mouth agape, she reached for the coffin-style violin case and slowly ran her fingers across the gilded burgundy covering. Lynn spoke without generality, "Look at this handcrafted case. The leather is brittle, and the hinges and handle are loose. I should buy a new case so I can preserve this one. It has traveled far and wide and is as much a piece of history as the violin."

Lynn paused in reverence and cautiously opened the case. "It's not a Stradivarius, but it certainly comes in a close second. Look at the quality of craftsmanship. The wood is well preserved; even the strings are intact. Remarkable!"

"What kind is it?" Trudy was leaning in to get a better look.

"It's a Guarneri. One sold at auction last year, and it fetched 15 million dollars. Its Holocaust provenance is significant. Look, Trudy, there's a message in German. Can you translate for us?"

"My name is Alma Rose, and I'm leaving my pride and joy violin here because I know the Nazis will be coming to take me to Auschwitz. Whoever finds this violin, please hold it dear to your heart and play, play, play."

"Trudy, didn't Ernst tell you anything about this woman? I'm so curious," said Penny.

"This is what I know: Alma was able to get her father to England, but they didn't have enough money to survive. He had been the conductor of the Vienna Symphony for fifty years. Now her father was too old to concertize, and no one wanted lessons. Alma went to Holland to find work, and the Nazis told her they would let her leave from a location in Germany. When Alma returned to Germany, she delivered her violin to Ernst because she was afraid, and rightly so. She planned to flee to Switzerland; however, the Gestapo picked her up in Berlin and shuttled her to Drancy, where she was imprisoned for several months before being taken to Auschwitz. She played the violin in a women's orchestra there, where she served as its conductor. She was also the capo for the Nazis. One night, her captors invited her to dinner. She fell ill and died. Ernst thought the Nazis poisoned her. The official report stated Alma Rose died of food poisoning."

"Oh, how horrible," said Lynn. "I certainly will treat her violin with great care. It will be an honor to play it."

Lynn picked up the instrument, wiped off the dust, and began to play. She stopped and declared, "I am going to name this violin Alma Rose."

"What a lovely gesture. You are a lucky young lady, Lynn. I believe Ernst must have been thinking about you after he heard you play." Trudy told them. "I had another idea. I think we should honor this house's heritage and have a plaque made that tells the property's history. It might even up the ante on the selling price."

"Trudy, is that being mercenary?" Penny quipped.

"Of course not, Penny. It will give the property provenance and be a tribute to Ernst. We should have engraved signage for the wall which will tell about Ernst and the history of this violin."

"When you put it that way, it is the right thing to do. We must preserve history. Do you have any ideas?"

"Let's call it 'Haus du Violine.' When Lynn goes with Tom to sign the real estate contract, we need them to use that name."

"I love the idea," said Lynn. "'Haus du Violine.' Maybe the gardener could trim the bushes out front so they would look like a violin."

"How very clever, Lynn. I'll talk to the gardener tomorrow. If he can't do it with greenery, maybe we could do it in the front flower bed."

Jean-Luc arrived and plopped down in the living room. "I'm tired and thirsty. There's some iced Kabinett in the refrigerator. Anyone besides me want a glass?"

"I'll get everything," said Tom as he walked toward the kitchen. "I'm the only one around here who hasn't been involved in hard labor." He laughed. "Negotiating is very tiring on the brain, though."

Everyone chuckled at his comment.

"Trudy, could you find us a sign maker that could make a metal sign saying 'Haus du Violine' and also carve a violin shape into the metal?"

"I probably could, but I think you should first ask the realtor."

"Good idea." Jean-Luc popped up out of his lethargy.

"Lynn, who are you going to use to sell the property?"

"The second firm we met. Tom and I agree, they will probably be the most aggressive in selling it. But I did like the other two people we spoke with also. They are coming over tomorrow morning to view the house."

"Did they give you some idea of the price?"

"I wouldn't expect Lynn to receive less than ten million American, maybe more because of the construction boom in East Berlin. It's the up-and-coming area."

Tom opened the second bottle of wine and filled everyone's glasses again. How about sauerbraten and red cabbage for dinner? The people we spoke to this afternoon told us about a great place for authentic German food."

"Sounds good. I'm getting hungry. How about you, Adrian?" Jean-Luc looked at his friend.

"My stomach is ready for anything. Good German food and a great beer. Lead the way!"

21

Since the others were off traveling, Ursula was the ideal mark to follow.

"Get that old biddy to tell you as much as she can about the family. Beat it out of her if you have to. I don't care what lengths you have to go to." Tennent barked orders.

Tennent's minion, Bernie the Rat, not because he was a snitch, but because he had a rat face, had been keeping a lookout on her. He parked down the street and watched a mover unload boxes from a station wagon that had seen better days. Thinking he might learn something, he approached Ursula and offered to lend a hand.

"Those boxes look heavy. Could I carry some of them for you?"

"You are so kind. I would appreciate it so much. I can't pay you very much, though."

"No problem," the stranger said.

Ursula accepted the stranger's offer to use his large sedan to get the last few boxes. He drove her back to Hilltop to retrieve the remainder of her belongings. As he approached the Hilltop entrance, the man's heart pumped faster. He felt his adrenaline spike when the gates swung open.

Ursula invited him into the kitchen, and while she was in her quarters, he took it upon himself to roam around the rest of the house. *A lot of stuff I think could be easily fenced. I bet some of it is pretty expensive.* The stranger didn't know where to look first. He placed a hushed call to Tennent to report his findings.

"Case the joint and grab what you can, then get out of there. Be quick about it. Lickety-split, dawg, so you can get the old lady back to her digs. If you see any nice paintings on the wall, take them."

Ursula found the man standing in the living room whispering on the phone. "What are you doing?" She was upset that the stranger had left the kitchen. "You were only invited into the kitchen."

It was then he knocked her out with a bronze statue from an end table. He grabbed whatever silver he could find and lifted a few paintings off the walls. Out of sheer meanness, he slashed the sofa and matching chairs with a butcher knife. Satisfied with the destruction, he carried the comatose housekeeper to his car. Once he got her and the rest of her belongings into the new apartment, he reached for a phone cord and wrapped it around her neck.

Ursula's eyes bulged wide. She tried to wrap her fingers around the cord to free herself, to no avail. The taut cord kept her from speaking, causing her to gasp for air. The attacker pulled the cord tighter and tighter. When she stopped moving, he dropped her limp body on the floor.

22

"It should be a few days before someone discovers her body, boss. I'll need to find another car, though."

"You did yourself proud, Bernie," said Tennent as he eyed the valuables Rat managed to steal. "Where are you going to fence the silver? I'll take care of the paintings."

"There's a guy on West Pico in L.A. I like to use. But my car could cause problems because I saw cameras all over the grounds."

"You didn't see any inside, did you?"

"Nah, boss. Just on the gate. She pushed a button, and they opened. Hell, I should have taken that remote with me."

"I think it's too late to retrieve it. Let's just hope you're not on any surveillance footage."

Bernie, Bernie, Bernie, you have no idea what you stole. I'm going to put you out of the picture, hawk the silver and sell the Driscoll to the highest bidder. What would be the easiest way to eliminate you?

Tennent knew if he wanted to dispose of Rat's body, he would have to dispose of the car first. Sending it off a cliff to a fiery grave might be the best way. *But where and when? And could I get Deke to pick me up? He may not do it, so I need a backup plan. Maybe just getting*

him arrested would be a better idea. I'll stew on it tonight.
Thoughts swirled around in the gangster's brain.

"Bernie, you did such a great job. Let me treat you to a hearty steak dinner tonight. How does that sound?"

"I can already taste it. Charred, blood-rare. And an ice cold beer to go with it."

"Whatever you want, for your pleasure. Let's drop your buggy off at the chop shop this afternoon. Joey 'Knuckles' should be able to dispose of it. I'll follow you there, and then we'll go for that steak."

"Sounds like a plan."

After his minion left, Tennent made a phone call. "I am in possession of a Maud Driscoll painting. It was done in the Napa Valley. Are you interested?"

"Always. How much do you want to part with it?"

"It should sell for around a quarter mil at least in your gallery. Maybe a lot more since the artist is dead and the paintings are rare."

"I can only give you one hundred. I don't want to deal in a stolen Driscoll."

"If you place it right, you won't have a problem. Not enough money, though. Think about it, my friend. You have my phone number."

Tennent disconnected from his call and placed another. The same conversation ensued. But the person on the other end of the line offered more money. "Where do you want me to deliver it?"

"My gallery in Beverly Hills. Can you do it before the gallery closes?"

"After hours, please. Do you want to do it tonight?"

"I have some uncrating to do. I'll be in the gallery until nine if that's okay. If I am interested, I will need to get it authenticated. One cannot be too careful."

"Perfect, see you then."

Once they hung up, the buyer put in a call to Lottie Wasserman. "Dr. Wasserman, this is Payton from the Beverly Hills Art Gallery."

"Hello Payton, how are you?"

Once the niceties were exchanged, "How can I help you, Payton?"

"I am in contact with someone who needs to dispose of a Maud Driscoll painting."

"Unreal. Do you know the subject?"

"I haven't seen it yet, but I'm told it was painted in the Napa Valley. Are you interested?"

"I'm always interested in a Driscoll. Do you want to bring it out to my house?"

"That would be my pleasure. How about this Sunday afternoon around two?"

"I'll look forward to seeing you and the painting. Thanks for calling me."

Lottie greeted her visitor at the door. He walked in and strode toward the living room with the painting under his arm.

"It is of the Napa Valley." She studied the painting carefully. "Payton, where did you get this?"

"From one of my suppliers. I told him I needed it to be authenticated, and he loaned it to me for a few days. Why?"

"I know this painting and the person who owns it. She would never give it up. It was a gift from some very dear friends. In fact, the son and daughter-in-law of Maud Driscoll. She does not want to sell this artwork."

"I didn't get it from a woman. It was a man. What are you telling me?"

"This painting has been stolen. I know it has. I'm confident you had no idea. The owner is in Europe at present. She's not expected back until sometime later this week."

"What should I do?"

"We need to call the police. I'm going to have someone guard it here until Trudy returns. Who is trying to sell the painting?"

"Bill Tennent, Tennent Galleries."

"Oh my god, Payton. He has been a nemesis to this family for years. You don't want to be involved with him at all. You could be held as an accomplice. That felon did time and was released from prison about three months ago."

Payton sat down in the nearest chair. Visibly shaken, his forehead glistened with beads of sweat. "That's why I haven't heard from him. I thought he was still at the Tennent Galleries."

"No, Avery let him go years ago."

"He fooled me. I'm so sorry, Dr. Wasserman."

Lottie called the Los Angeles Police Department and asked for the detective bureau. Once she explained the situation, Detective Harley Bronson was on her doorstep in thirty minutes.

"Mr. Payton, you may have to give Tennent some money just to hold him at bay. I want to go see the King residence in Laguna Beach and take a look around."

"I told Tennent I'd give him $200,000 for the painting. I don't keep that kind of money at the gallery."

"Can you hold him off for a few days?"

"I can try."

"Here is my phone number. If you have any problems asking for 48 hours to come up with the cash, call me at once." Bronson's excitement was visible when he realized he almost had Tennent in his grasp.

Knowing the crime occurred outside his jurisdiction, Bronson called the Laguna police to ask for assistance. The two detectives met at the King residence and surveyed the damage to Trudy's living room.

"It looks like there was some kind of struggle," said Max Dedham, the Laguna detective.

"Where's the housekeeper who lives here?"

A thorough search of the house revealed nothing but more damage. One of the detectives noticed a piece of paper on the kitchen floor. He picked it up to see a Laguna

Beach address was written on it. "Think we should go check this out."

The two detectives arrived at the apartment Ursula had rented. The door was unlocked. They went in and found a woman's body on the floor. "It looks like she's been dead a few days."

Max summoned the coroner, and the forensic unit arrived to photograph and dust for fingerprints.

"I sure opened a can of worms. I had no idea a painting would lead to such death and destruction." Harley and Max stood talking while they watched the body being removed from the premises.

"This time, Bill Tennent will be going behind bars for good. He has wreaked havoc on this family and their friends over the years. He is bent on stealing Driscoll paintings and harbors contempt for Penny Wells in particular."

"We've been keeping an eye on him and know he's got to have an accomplice. He hasn't moved from his apartment except to buy groceries or go out to eat."

"Wherever Mrs. King is, we need to get her back to Laguna as soon as possible. I hate giving bad news like this over the phone."

"Maybe we can find out some information in a calendar, date-book, or the deceased's cell phone. Can your boys handle the search in quick order? Time is of the essence in this case."

"Not a problem. I guess we should officially introduce ourselves since I think this will be a joint investigation. I'm Max Dedham," said the Laguna detective.

"Harley Bronson, L.A.'s finest." They both laughed.

"Max, I'm going to call the airlines and see what planes are scheduled to return from Europe. Someone must be picking her up at the airport and returning her to Laguna."

23

"Mr. Tennent, this is Payton. My client says she will buy the painting, but she needs 48 hours to sell some stock to pay for it. If you want to come to the gallery Thursday afternoon, I will have the money for you."

"Can't you get it sooner?" A whiny tone sounded from his mouth.

"I asked, not possible."

"Well, I guess it will have to do. See you Thursday afternoon."

He hung up and immediately called Bernie the Rat, catching him on his way into a pawn shop. "Hey, good news, my guy will pay me ten big ones for the painting. Now we really must celebrate." Tennent could hear drooling on the other end of the line. *I'm lucky that insipid fool knows nothing about art. I'll make a cleaning on the proceeds.*

Bernie had a private appointment with a pawnbroker. "I can give you $500 for the whole lot, Bernie." The proprietor surveyed the items. "Silver just doesn't sell anymore. You might want to try a flea market."

"I just wanna get rid of the stuff." He emptied the rest of the pieces he had brought with him on the counter.

After they left West Pico Antiques, Tennent suggested they stop for a drink before they went to dinner.

"Fine by me, Tennent. A beer would taste good right now."

"There's a couple of used car places on the left. Maybe we could find you a car. And I agree, a beer would taste damn good."

Tennent was brewing a scheme in his mind. *I have a great idea. I should give Rat my car after I take care of my little Wells problem in Pasadena. I've been casing the joint for weeks, and nobody suspects a thing. She's been gone two, and now she's back. Walks her dog every day at the same time. She won't finish that next walk, by God. They'll pick up Bernie instead of me because I gave him the car.*

24

"Trudy, you don't mind traveling with Lynn? Tom will take good care of the two of you. I need to leave on an earlier plane to return to the museum," said Penny. "I want to be there to receive the shipment. There's a flight out tomorrow morning. I'll leave you gentlemen to take care of the shipment."

Adrian looked over the packed items and checked each entry against the inventory list. It seemed like the number of boxes would never end. "Penny is going to have an absolute ball opening all these crates."

She called the museum director and read some of the entries on the manifesto. His response was, "OMG! Penny, you struck the mother lode! We both know you want to retire, but I hope you will stay on until after the exhibition."

"Without a doubt. This viewing will be an amazing triumph for me to cap off my career."

"What will you do when you arrive in Los Angeles?" Trudy wanted Adrian to tell her all the details.

"The Los Angeles County Museum of Art is sending a truck and guard to the airport. We will see that everything is back to the museum in good order. Jean-Luc and I will stay at a hotel near the museum and we'll rent a car. I am looking forward to seeing Hilltop. Jean-Luc has described it to me. It sounds beautiful."

"It is Adrian. It's my paradise on earth. It always amazed me how my life changed when I met Penny in a hallway at the Waldorf Astoria Hotel many years ago. It's because of her I moved to California. I always thought that once I left Berlin, New York would be the only place to live. To me, Berlin will always be cold and ugly even though it's the city is having a renaissance. My old home was torn down. It was an ugly behemoth, and now a tall-towered building stands in its place. I just think of cold and unhappiness and the war. The only reason I'm here now is because of Lynn. She's like a daughter to me, and I would do everything and anything to honor Ernst's wishes."

"He must have been an incredible man."

"He was an unsung hero. His underground railroad helped save many Jews from persecution by getting them out of Germany, into Switzerland, and beyond. Ernst bid safe passage to those who departed, worried about their fate. He retained the prized possessions he was given in payment but never did think of the heirlooms as payment, though. He planned to keep the treasures safe until the families returned someday. All that remains of some of the victims are their shoes, memorialized, and on display at the United States Holocaust Memorial Museum. Some shoes belonged to infants. Heartbreaking."

Adrian was choked with emotion. "I know what you, Jean-Luc, Penny, and Ernst did to return many pieces of art to their rightful owners. Maybe you will be able to find more heirs."

"That would be an extra star in the crown Ernst already has."

25

The Los Angeles detectives worked overtime to determine when Trudy would be returning to Laguna. Max thought a woman of her stature might not make the reservations herself and probably employed a travel agency's services. He asked a clerk at his station to find the name and phone number of all Laguna agencies. He knew it was a long shot, but it was worth a try. The first three phone numbers on the list were a dead end. On the fourth call, he hit pay dirt. "I'll be in your office in about ten minutes."

"Hello, I'm Max Dedham, Senior Detective of the Laguna Police Department." He shook hands with the attractive woman he had spoken with previously.

"Trudy King is a personal friend of mine and one of our best clients. How can I help you?" She invited Max to sit in the chair across from her desk.

"Were you acquainted with Ursula Becker?"

"Yes. She is Trudy's oldest friend. In 1938, Ursula started working for Trudy in West Berlin. She was much more than a housekeeper, though, and did everything from cooking to cleaning. Ursula has a reputation for being one of the finest cooks anywhere."

"I have terrible news, ma'am. Miss Becker was murdered two days ago. Mrs. King's house was burglarized and torn to shreds. Many items are missing, but we do not know the extent until Trudy comes home. A famous Driscoll painting was stolen, too."

The agent's face reddened as she burst into tears. She pulled out a box of Kleenex from her side drawer and dabbed her eyes. "Why would anyone want to hurt a person as dear as Ursula? She was a treasure among treasures."

"Right now, all I can say is she was in the wrong place at the wrong time. We are just beginning to piece the evidence together. Do you know where Mrs. King was going and when she is returning?" The detective took out his small spiral pad to take notes.

Through gulping sobs, the woman told the detective all she knew. "Trudy took Aisalynn, the young woman who lives with her, to Berlin. Her last name is Sheperd. That is spelled S-H-E-P-E-R-D. She is a talented, up-and-coming violinist. In fact, she just played with the San Francisco Symphony a few weeks ago. After the performance, a homeless person standing outside the stage door sliced her neck. I think the attacker was still on the loose."

"Is she all right?"

"Yes, she is physically, but the attack rocked her to the core. They believe it was the act of someone who has been harassing them for years, and that person of interest put a contract out on her life. The police are certain it wasn't Lynn the man was intent on hurting. It was Penny Wells, Trudy King's friend. She was standing next to Lynn when the attack occurred. Can you tell me about the others Trudy is acquainted with?"

"I booked their trip to Berlin. I can give you their names: Penny Wells is the senior curator at the LACMA. Jean-Luc Troyer is a friend, gallery owner, and appraiser. Lavinia and Dr. Michel Troyer are Penny's cousins, he by marriage. Michel is Jean-Luc's twin brother. A lawyer went with them, Thomas Worley. I understand he represents Lynn and the Weber estate."

"Do you know when they are returning?"

"I am not sure. Trudy changed her itinerary. I can call the airlines and find out if it would help you."

"Absolutely." Max picked up a business card from the holder in front of him and looked at the embossed name. "Thank you, Lydia." He handed her his card and wrote down his cell phone number on the back.

"I'll call you as soon as I have more information."
She weakly smiled. Ursula's passing left sadness in her
eyes.

"I appreciate that. You can call me day or night.
We want to get this murder and robbery solved. Mrs.
King's home is an absolute mess. I hope she had some
before pictures for insurance purposes. She is going to
need it."

Max put in a call to Harley and told him what
transpired at the travel agency.

"That's great. We've just reviewed the security
footage from the cameras on the property. Seems we have
our perp. He is no stranger to the system, and we are well
acquainted with him, Bernie 'the Rat' Landon. Do you
recognize the name, Max? He shared a cell with Tennent
for a couple of years at Folsom. He doesn't have much
upstairs, so I think it was easy for Tennent to get him to
do his dirty work."

Harley recalled, "Landon wasn't one of the thieves
we captured from the gallery theft. The guy we nabbed
was Tennent's good buddy, Deke something or other,
don't remember his last name."

"I was told he picked up Tennent at the prison when he was released. Deke's parole officer told me Deke had gone straight and probably would do nothing to help Tennent's criminal enterprise. But we will check him out as you can imagine."

26

In a sleazy San Fernando Valley motel, a crazed Bill
Tennent sat drinking an expensive bottle of champagne. "I
did it! Oh boy, did I ever! I got some revenge on Penny
Wells by knifing her famous musician friend and offing
that old housekeeper. And I'm still not done shaking that
bitch down. Her day will come. I don't care if I get
caught; well, yeah, I do. It is time to change my looks
again and get out of town. Maybe I'll go to Thailand. I've
read about all the cosmetic surgery they do. Hell, a lot
cheaper than L.A."

Tennent toasted his reflection in the mirror. "If I
have food and supplies delivered, I won't be seen on the
street. I think now is a good time to call Bernie and give
him my car. I think that's a genius solution. My car has
been seen all around that pompous bitch's neighborhood.
They'll follow and arrest Rat. Good idea, Tennent. Now
you're thinking!"

"Hey Rat, You wanna you come over and take my
car? I'm not feeling so hot, or else I would drive it to you.
I have some business out of state, and I don't know when

I'll be returning." *That ought to be enough info for that simpleton. He doesn't ask too many questions, and I did give him five g's.*

"Sure, boss. When do you want me to come and get it?" The ex-con was thrilled thinking about the restored black Caddie with fishtails. *I'll be drivin' in style.*

It was dark when Tennent heard a knock at the door.

"Hey man, thanks for helping me out and taking care of my car," Tennent answered the door in undershorts and a torn tee shirt. Unshaven, he had a sickly appearance.

"You look like hell, Tennent. What's wrong?"

"Just my stomach. I think it is something I ate. I'll be okay." Tennent walked over to the kitchen counter, picked up the keys, and handed over the Cadillac title.

"Here you are; enjoy it in good health." *I don't think you'll be on the outside much longer.* "Make sure you close the door after you take the car out. It's garage E."

"Will do, boss. And gee, thanks. You're a swell guy."

Bernie was smiling ear to ear when he left Tennent's and pulled the car out of the garage. He drove his new possession off into the night, oblivious another vehicle was following him.

"With the trunk wiped clean of fingerprints and my prints off the steering wheel and doors, you're going to be in hot water for the Wells murder, you stupid fool. That will give me just enough time to give myself a makeover and scram outta Dodge," Tennent said to himself.

Tennent dyed his hair black, slicked it back with gel, stuffed a pillow into an oversized pair of trousers, put on a shirt and tie, and a coat that was twice the usual size. His outward persona became one of a plump, jolly man. The mirror showed him what he wanted to see. "I think I look like a midwestern salesman. Yep, I sell machine parts. Where's my driver's license? Got my burner phone and now to dispose of anything that might indicate I changed my appearance. I cleaned out my bank account. The money is in my carry-on. I'll first take a flight to Chicago from Burbank. Then I'll book for someplace warm, Mexico? Southern France, Fiji?" He stared into the mirror. "What's my name now? You're looking at Leonard Bertram. Friends call me Leon." He gave the mirror a weird smile. Tennent fit an appliance around his gums to give his mouth a drooped look. He approved of the new look and walked two streets away to a small bar.

"I'll take a draft beer," he said to the bartender as he slid onto the barstool.

"That really hit the spot." He wiped the foam from his upper lip on his sleeve and ordered another. "The name's Leon Bertram. Where am I exactly? This territory is all new to me. I think I might need a taxi. Can I get one here?"

"Sure, Leon, give me a sec, and I'll call one for you. Where you from?"

"Iowa mostly, and Ohio. I sell machine parts. I'm several days late for getting back to my wife. It's our anniversary. She's going to be mighty mad at me."

"There's an airport a few miles away. Maybe you could get a flight out tonight or early morning." Solicitous of his patron, the bartender went out of his way to be helpful.

"Good idea, what airport?"

"Ask the cabbie to take you to the Burbank airport."

27

"Burbank Airport," Tennent told the cabbie. *I'm rollin' now, baby.* Once he arrived at the airport, he went to the nearest ticket counter and asked if they had a flight to Chicago.

"We have a flight leaving for O'Hare in about an hour. I have two seats left."

"I only need one. Thanks a million." Tennent handed the reservation clerk his Leonard Bertram driver's license and paid in cash for the ticket. "Which way do I go, Miss?"

"Down the corridor to the very last gate."

An hour later, Tennent was flying above Burbank on his way to the windy city. He sat back in his seat and relaxed. The steward bought him a scotch on the rocks, which helped him relax even more.

Once he deplaned, he took a taxi to a small upscale hotel and engaged a room. He called the concierge and asked for a men's store with an employee who would come to the hotel. Tennent shed the pillow and the oversized clothing and put on the complimentary hotel robe he found in the closet. Room service delivered the lunch he ordered while waiting for the clothier to arrive.

"I'll take that dark gray suit. How about a blue shirt and a gray and blue tie? That should look good with the suit. I want a couple of pairs of slacks and two shirts, a matching sports coat and I'll need underwear and socks. Oh, and a belt, don't forget a belt. Do you sell luggage?"

Tennent enjoyed barking orders to the sales clerk. "If you will total everything up, I'll give you cash for my purchases. When you select the suitcase, I want a dark brown one with wheels. Make sure it is lightweight and large enough to hold the suits. Can you bring it back here tonight?"

"Yes, of course, Mr. Bertram."

After the purchases were delivered, Tennent packed the suitcase, keeping one outfit aside. The next morning, he realized he needed some shaving equipment, personal essentials, and a new pair of shoes. After downing a quick cup of coffee, Tennent went to the shops lining the concourse and found a shoe store. He then headed down the block to a pharmacy. As he was returning to his hotel, he spotted a travel agency and went inside. He studied the brochure display before making up his mind.

"I'd like to purchase a ticket to Mexico City. I want an open-ended return because I don't know where I want to go after that. I'm joining some friends, and they have asked me to travel with them. Can I get a ticket like that?"

"Of course. You'll leave Chicago tomorrow morning. Fly to Houston and then on to Mexico."

"Sounds great. It will be the first time I've been there."

"Is your passport in order?"

That little question stunned Tennent. He had not thought about a passport. *I'll have to find someone to forge me a passport. Who do I know in Chicago?*

"I'll have to dig up my passport. My ex-wife might have it at her house. Do you have a flight a day or two later?" Tennent became very glib in his lies.

Tiny something or other…what the heck is his name? Very unusual last name. Tennent was trying to recall the forger. *Said his brother-in-law had a bar somewhere in the Chicago loop. Guess I'll have to go bar hopping today.*

He was surprised when he entered the second bar. Tiny came up and said, "Hey, Tennent."

"Tiny, you're not going to believe this, but you are exactly the person I'm looking for. Let's go sit in that corner booth and talk." Once seated and a beer placed in front of each of them, Tennent told Tiny he needed a passport with a different name, and he had a one-way ticket to Mexico City the day after tomorrow.

"It's gonna cost ya."

"How much? Can I get it by tomorrow afternoon?"

"That's no problem. That'll be $1500 good hard cash."

"Here's $500 to get the ball rolling," said Tennent as he peeled off five one hundred dollar bills and put them in Tiny's hand. "I'll give you the rest when I have the passport tomorrow afternoon."

The two men shook hands. "Oh, and the name you use is Leonard Bertram. Do you need the spelling?"

"Write it down on this napkin." Tiny stuffed the white bar napkin in his pocket.

28

The detectives had put a stakeout on Tennent's apartment in Los Angeles. For twenty-four hours, there had been no movement inside or out. The next shift checked the garage and saw that the black Cadillac was gone. They went up to his apartment and discovered the door was unlocked and entered.

"This place is cleaned out. Only a few clothes are hanging in the closet, and the fridge is empty. It looks like nothing has been touched in days. I wonder where the hell he went."

"Don't know," said his partner, "but I want to contact Harley and tell him what we found. No Tennent and no car."

Harley informed the officers, "Someone was seen driving Tennent's car last night. One of your team followed him to an apartment complex in Reseda's run-down area and went inside a downstairs unit. We identified pictures of the driver. It was Bernie Landon. He's been a minion for Tennent ever since they met while serving time at Folsom."

"Should we go pick him up?"

"Not yet," said Harley, "we want to see if he makes contact with Tennent."

"Tennent appears to have vanished. Some clothes are in the closet. Even his toothbrush sat on the bathroom sink. Do you think Landon might have killed him?"

"I think it would be the other way around, but I've been surprised before. Landon is more than a little light on brain cells. Wait for another twenty-four hours before you pick him up. But do follow him. You can end the watch on Tennent. We will find him, though. Keep me posted, fellas."

Harley called Max to discuss the case. "I think Landon may have committed the robbery and murder of Miss Becker. Send his pic to my cell phone so that I can compare it with the man on the King cameras."

"That's our man. Go pick him up. Read him his rights and bring that Caddie to the lab. I want forensics to go over it with a fine-tooth comb." Harley felt an adrenaline rush.

Bernie was living high off the hog, spending the money Tennent had given him. Surprised by the two officers that arrived at his front door, he didn't put up any barriers when they cuffed him and ushered him to the back of the police car. He was driven to the Los Angeles Police Department's main headquarters and placed in an interrogation room with Max and Harley.

"What did I do?"

"We have your mug on tape at the Gertrude King home in Laguna, carrying out a painting and some silver."

"I was only doing what my friend asked me to do."

"Who's the friend?"

"My best friend, Bill Tennent." Bernie was all smiles when he told the interrogator.

"Why would he tell you to do that?"

"He wanted the painting on the wall. He gave me $5000 for it." Landon puffed up his chest, proud of the fact he made so much money.

"That stoolie has no idea he lifted a priceless painting," Harley leaned over and whispered to Max.

"What else did he tell you?" The detectives couldn't wait to hear the answer.

"He told me to help myself to whatever I wanted. All that silver was so shiny and purty. I thought it would give me a lot of money if I sold it."

"What about the elderly woman who lived there?" Max waited for his answer.

"I helped her move into this apartment. She was a nice old gal but told me she didn't have any money to pay me. I thought that would be okay since I was going to take the silver."

"Did she know that?" One of the detectives asked.

"I don't know, but I did take her to her apartment and help her move in her stuff."

"What else did you do?"

"What do you mean? Nothin', I didn't do nothin' else."

"Your prints were all over the cell phone cord you strangled her with."

"I didn't hurt her. I helped her."

"How did you do that?"

"I let her sleep."

"Your definition of sleep and ours is a bit different. Bernard Landon, I am charging you with the murder of Ursula Becker and the robbery of the Gertrude King home."

Bernie's mind wasn't quick enough to understand the implications. "Can I go now?"

"No, Bernie. The state is going to be housing you for a long time. You may never see the world without steel bars in between."

Bernie looked at him. "Where's my friend?"

"That's what we'd like to know."

"He gave me his car. Told me he had some out-of-town business. Didn't know when he would be coming back to L.A."

"Guard, take Mr. Landon to a cell."

Harley and Max compared notes. "He's slipped out of L.A. somehow. Mrs. King thought he had disguised himself and came to her gallery once or twice. We'll find him, Harley." Max was disgusted for having Tennent slip through their fingers.

"So, he may have changed his appearance, name, and whatever else to disguise himself. Where would he go?" Harley sat thinking, pushing a pencil up and down on the table.

"Wherever he went, we will find him. He had to have taken a taxi somewhere. We'll check every business on the streets where he kept an apartment. Someone must have seen him. Do you want to do this with me? I know Tennent's in L.A.'s jurisdiction, but part of the crime occurred in Orange County. I'd be glad to do this jointly until we close the books on this case."

The two detectives were dogged in their search. They returned to a bar where Tennent frequented and interviewed the staff and patrons at different hours of the day and night, showing Tennent's picture to everyone.

One night the detectives approached a bartender they hadn't encountered before. Max and Harley flashed their badges and sat down. "Say," said Harley, "have you seen this guy around?" He slapped a picture of Tennent on the bar.

"Not for a couple of weeks. Maybe two, three weeks ago."

The detectives stood to leave when the bartender called to them. "Come to think of it, there was a strange fella in here about a week ago. Fat, wore glasses. Said he needed to get to the airport. I got him a taxi, a yellow cab."

Max's eyes lit up. "I think we might have caught our first break. Let's find out what cab company and where he took the mystery man. Mrs. King arrives at LAX tomorrow. We should be there to soften the blow. What difficult news we to have to tell her."

29

Trudy deplaned with Tom and Lynn. The Berlin climate made Trudy's arthritis flare and she was in obvious pain. Tom held on to her gently but with great care. The limo was waiting on the tarmac to return them to Pasadena and then Laguna. Awaiting their arrival at the foot of the stairs were Harley and Max.

"My goodness, a reception, Tom. Did you plan this?"

"No, Trudy, but I believe those men are police detectives and not men from my firm."

"Oh, this is not good. Do you think some of the paintings or artifacts were stolen?"

"Mrs. King, my name is Max Dedham. I'm a senior detective with the Laguna Beach Police Department. This is Harley Bronson with the Los Angeles Police Department. She acknowledged the introductions and waited for him to say more based on the serious tone. "Would you like to sit in your limo?" Max was equally concerned, despite his gruff manner.

"Yes, of course." She followed them to the car and stepped inside. "How can I help you, detectives?"

"Mrs. King, while you were in Europe, your home was vandalized and robbed. Several items were stolen. We believe all the items have been recovered, and we have apprehended a suspect. The evidence is stacked against him." Max said.

Harley added, "Your living room is in shambles. But that isn't the worst of it. I'm so sorry to tell you your friend Ursula Becker has been murdered."

Trudy keened. "No, no, it can't be! She never hurt anyone in her life." Trudy sobbed uncontrollably. Once she composed herself, she looked at the detectives for information.

"She was found in her apartment. The coroner reported she had been dead for a couple of days. Other occupants of the building told us about a man who helped her move. We believe he is the culprit."

"It's not William Tennent, is it?"

"No, but we believe he is the mastermind."

"Does Penny Wells know?"

"I've spoken to Mr. Troyer. He will tell her."

30

"Tom, where are Jean-Luc and Penny?"

"Penny is home in Pasadena, and Jean-Luc and Adrian are back in Laguna. I was told the cargo had been safely delivered to the museum. I can have Jean-Luc meet us at Hilltop if you would like."

"Please, Tom, I'm afraid I might fall apart. I'm devastated by Ursula's death. Losing her so senselessly is a terrible blow. I can't believe it. We survived the Nazis, for goodness sake, and she meets her demise like this?"

Sunday morning, Trudy received another earth-shattering blow. Just an hour after the police told Trudy about Ursula, Penny was rushed to the hospital and in critical condition due to a brutal knife attack. The *L.A. Times* had an article, accompanied by Penny's stock photo from a gala she once attended.

Dr. Lottie Wasserman and thousands of other

readers opened their Sunday morning paper to learn what had happened. Thunderstruck, she sat down in her sunroom with a cup of coffee in hand as she read the horrific news about the attack on Penny. The fact that Penny was still alive was a miracle.

The front page article stated:

Penelope Maud Wells, recently divorced from Petros Petros, a Greek shipping magnate and real estate tycoon, was found brutally stabbed on the front lawn of her home on South Orange Grove in Pasadena.

A bodyguard was also wounded in the attack and a hospital spokesperson said he is in critical condition but is expected to survive. Well's dog sat beside her owner, keeping watch.

Neighbors reported seeing a black late-model sedan driving around the neighborhood and reported hearing a car backfire before it sped off.

Ms. Wells has been senior curator for the Los Angeles County Museum of Art for over twenty years. She is the heiress to the Maud Driscoll and Peter Wells winery fortune. Driscoll, a famous artist, was her grandmother, and Wells, her father.

In the last month, she set up a foundation for the museum and funded it with over thirty million dollars to build a wing onto the museum to house the extensive Driscoll collection in her possession.

Ms. Wells is a founding member of The Reclamation Project, an international group of art lovers whose mission is to return art and artifacts stolen by the Nazis to their rightful heirs.

The police claim they know who the assailant is and an all-points-bulletin has been issued.

Tears streamed down Lottie's face as she thought about all the selfless acts Penny had done for her. She helped reunite her with Ernst and their family painting, thought gone forever, was returned to her so many years after she left Berlin.

Once she could speak to Trudy without tearing up again, she called her friend. "Trudy, I'm dumbstruck. I just read about Penny in the *Times* article. Do you want me to come down and be with you?"

"Lottie, right now I'm in a complete fog. If Lynn

and Tom hadn't been here, I probably would have had a heart attack for sure. This, on top of Ursula's murder, has me falling apart at the seams. They won't let me visit Penny. She is under twenty-four-hour guard because the police believe Tennent will be back to try to complete his aborted attempt. I am a wreck and would love to have you here. Can you take time off from your practice?"

"You know I've semi-retired, so only see patients on Wednesday and Thursday. I could be there by this afternoon, stay for a couple of days and then return on Friday."

"That would be such a comfort to me. Tom and Jean-Luc are helping me prepare a memorial service for Ursula. We could use your input too. Thank you so much for offering to be here."

Trudy hung up her phone and wiped the newly formed tears away from her eyes. *Penny, Ursula, how will I live without my two friends? Ursula has always been a loyal friend and managed to keep me and the house so organized. I need to find a new housekeeper. I can't think about that now. Except I must. I don't cook. I can't even boil water. Bill Tennent, wherever you are, I know the police will find you soon, and you'll go to prison for life. You are lucky that executions are carried out by lethal injection. Even hanging would be too good for you!*

31

Tennent was ready to leave the hotel and head to the airport when he caught a glimpse of the newspaper headlines.

"Heiress Survives Vicious Attack." The article said that socialite Penny Wells is in a coma and listed in critical condition at a Los Angeles area hospital. The doctors are encouraged by her vitals but say it is too soon to know if she will survive.

"Son-of-a-bitch! I've got to get back there and finish the job. The cops are probably watching all the airports around Pasadena. It's safer for me to fly to Long Beach, rent a car and finish the job. I can drive back to Long Beach and take off from there."

32

Lynn had no more concerts scheduled for the summer. She played the Guarneri and loved the sonorous tones it gave. "What a joy to play," she said every time she picked up the violin.

Since Penny had been injured so severely, Lynn felt it necessary to speak with the museum director about all the artwork and artifacts delivered there. Once she made the initial contact with the director, the two set up a meeting time and date. Tom volunteered to accompany her.

"Anything I can do to help, my darling. Maybe we can have dinner afterward and you can spend the night at my place rather than driving back to Laguna."

"You're probably right." As Lynn spoke with him, she knew she had to tell him about the concert tour position the Maestro offered her. She didn't think he would be pleased about it, although she was over the moon with excitement.

Once they arrived at Tom's condo, Lynn asked to freshen up and then be ready to go for dinner.

"We can walk over to Lake Avenue if you like. The weather is beautiful and balmy."

"I'd like that, Tom. Let me just put the finishing touches on my face," she said as she applied a tulip-pink lipstick.

"How about walking over to the Chronicle? Then we can window shop on the way back." Tom could see Lynn smiling once he mentioned window shop. He didn't even have to look at her expression.

The Chronicle was packed as usual, but Tom saw the owner who told him to sit at the bar, have a drink, and his table would be ready. "Give them what they want. It's on me," the owner said to the bartender.

Once they were seated in a plush corner booth, Lynn could feel her body relax, even though she dreaded her meaningful conversation with Tom.

"Let's, talk about the wedding, honey. Do you want to be married at Christmas? Or is there any date that would suit you better?"

"Tom, my darling Tom. I am so torn about what I must tell you. The Maestro has offered me an incredible opportunity, a concert tour all over Europe. I don't want to turn him down. I can't. I have practiced my entire life for this exposure."

"Do you know in what cities you'll be playing?"

"All the major cities in the British Isles, Paris, Geneva, Vienna. I don't know all of them. I know there is one in Moscow and one in Stockholm. Can we get married, and you come with me for as long as you can as our honeymoon?"

Tom's face was one of huge disappointment. "I didn't realize what it meant to be married to a world-class violinist. Can't you stay in Pasadena and just play with the orchestras in the local area?"

"That's not what I trained all my life to do. If you want to be engaged for the year I will be traveling, I will wait. Or I could marry you tomorrow. I love you, Tom. I want to be your wife. But I need fulfillment of my life's dream too."

Tom's attitude was not what Lynn expected. He became contentious, downright nasty, and made remarks about her talent. He even criticized the Maestro. It was a flood of unkind comments she couldn't believe were spewing from his lips.

When their dinner arrived, Lynn pecked around her duck entrée, eating little. Her gay demeanor had diminished to sadness and Tom's was no better. They finished their meal in silence and did not order dessert. Tom solemnly paid the bill, and they left.

"I have a lot of work at the office tomorrow, Lynn. Do you think Trudy might be up at the hospital, and you could go back to Laguna with her?"

"Let's go see if anyone is there with Penny now. Don't worry about taking me back to Laguna. I can rent a car for the day. I certainly wouldn't want to interrupt your busy schedule."

Tom could hear the anger in Lynn's voice. Fortuitously, Lynn saw Jean-Luc just as he was leaving the hospital. A quick conversation and he agreed to gather her luggage from Tom's condo and take her back to Laguna. She rode with Jean-Luc to show him the way. Once Tom opened his front door, Lynn showed Jean-Luc her bags and he put them in the trunk of his car.

Tom was livid and refused a kiss. Lynn had never seen this side of him. She removed her engagement ring, set the diamond on the entry table and left with Jean-Luc.

"Why did you do that, Lynn? In Berlin, you two were inseparable."

"He wants me to give up my violin career. I can't live with that. I've worked and practiced since I was a child to reach this place. Now the Maestro is giving me the chance to soar to the pinnacle. And I want it. I want that brass ring. I won't let Tom stop me."

"Maybe he's a little jealous of your fame?"

"I don't know, Jean-Luc. But I've never seen him so angry. I couldn't live that way under his thumb. Marriage must be an equal partnership. I thought that was what Tom wanted. But he doesn't." Lynn's tears began to flow.

"You know what, Lynn. Just give it time. You two are both still young. You're twenty-six, yes?"

"Yes."

"And Tom is what, twenty-eight? He's at the beginning of his career. I'm sure he'll come around. He loves you too."

"I hope so, Jean-Luc." Lynn laid her head back and slept the entire drive home.

33

Trudy heard a car come up the drive. Not expecting anyone, she flicked on all the security lights, illuminating the front yard. When she saw Lynn and Jean-Luc, she opened the door and embraced her friends.

"Lynn, I didn't expect you until tomorrow. I thought Tom was returning you."

"Tom and I are no longer engaged." Lynn began crying again and ran to her room.

"Jean-Luc, what is going on?"

"Tom told Lynn he didn't want her to perform anywhere except around the Pasadena area. She could entertain friends and family, but not the world. Lynn didn't take kindly to that, as you can well imagine. Instead of spending the night at his house, she had him drop her off at the hospital to see Penny. I was just leaving the hospital when Lynn saw me. She asked me to take her back to Tom's to retrieve her luggage and drive her here."

"What about Tom?"

"He disappeared into his condo and slammed a door. Lynn set her engagement ring on the front hall table and we left."

"Poor baby. She must be heartbroken. I know she wants to concertize more than anything in the world. She should not have to choose between Tom and her violin. Tom must feel threatened to act like that."

"You have to remember, Lynn is strong-willed and stubborn like her German heritage. She will stand up for everything and anything she believes in. I'm for her one hundred and ten percent." Jean-Luc said to Trudy.

"I agree whole-heartedly. I'm certain, in time, there will be a compromise. Tom's firm is handling Lynn's affairs. That's going to become very sticky. Maybe Lynn will want me to act in her stead. If she does, will you help me, please?"

"Whatever you need, Trudy. Just ask. You didn't ask about Penny, though. Don't you want to hear how she is doing?"

"Tell me, is she awake?" Trudy's concern was visible. "My attention was so focused on Lynn I didn't think about Penny for the moment."

"Penny is awake. She is not alert yet. She sleeps for a bit, wakes up, turns her head, and then goes back to sleep. I didn't talk to her, but she knew I was holding her hand."

"What are the doctors saying? Will she recover completely?"

"Yes, she will recover, but it will take time. Do you have her dog?'

"I do. She's adorable, and I have to admit that pooch keeps me entertained."

"The hospital said we could take the dog to visit her. The doctor thought it might be a comfort to her."

"When I go up the day after tomorrow, I'll take Chouchen with me. I'm going to stay at Penny's for a couple of nights, so I don't have the long drive."

"Good idea. I'll come around and see Lynn or at least call her to make sure she is doing fine. If you are still looking for a housekeeper, I'm sure Lynn would not mind doing some interviewing. It would be good to get her mind off Tom."

"That's a good suggestion. Come over tomorrow for lunch, and we all will talk about it."

"See you then, Trudy, and thanks for making it lunch. I need some sleep. I'm exhausted."

Jean-Luc arrived at Hilltop the next afternoon to be greeted by a dancing Chouchen so happy to see him. Jean-Luc patted the little fluffy white dog and then turned to Lynn. "No phone call from Tom?"

"Nary a word. I guess it is really over. I need another lawyer. I will no longer use Tom as my attorney. I like the people at the firm, but do you think it's a bit much to leave my case there?"

"I am acquainted with one of the senior partners there. I can talk to him about the best way to extricate you from Tom. I'll ask him to meet me outside the office so I won't be subject to seeing him. The partner and his wife own a condo in an adjoining part of my complex, and I usually see him there on weekends. I'll call and ask."

"Jean-Luc, you are the best of the best."

"Why, thank you, Lynn."

At that moment, Trudy arrived at the doorway and asked why they all didn't come inside. Pleasant aromas were wafting from Trudy's dining room. Lunch was waiting even though it wasn't Ursula's fare.

"I bought it from a new French restaurant in town, and it smells quite divine."

"Lynn, what's next on your agenda? Jean-Luc reached over for another helping of the blanquette de veau. Will you be packing another suitcase soon?"

"That's what I need to talk to Trudy about. The Maestro called me this morning. He wants me to fly to Atlanta to play at an outdoor music festival. I won't be the soloist but will play in a quartet. It sounds like a fun appearance. It's scheduled for the end of the month. I would be gone for two, maybe three days. I'm so worried about Penny. I don't want to do anything until I know she's going to be okay."

"We are all worried about her, darling, but the doctors feel she is progressing nicely. I'm going up to stay at her place for a few days. I'll take Chou with me and bring her to visit Penny in the hospital. I think it will be good for both of them."

"Is she still being guarded? That horrible man is around somewhere, and I'm afraid he might try again. He's hell-bent on killing her." Lynn and Jean-Luc were both all ears to Trudy's words.

"The police haven't found him yet, but Penny will continue to have 'round-the-clock protection until Tennent is captured." Trudy stood. "Excuse me. I'm going to get another pitcher of iced tea."

"Lynn, it's my turn to ask a favor of you," said Trudy as she sat back down at the table and refilled everyone's glasses. You are painfully aware I don't cook. And you can't be spending your precious practice time in the kitchen. I want to place an ad in the local newspapers for a housekeeper, cook and all-around general assistant. I'd like you to begin interviewing them so I can spend more time with Penny. Can you do that for me?"

"Of course, I can, Trudy. We'll get the ads to the papers today, and I'm sure it won't be long before we can find someone. No one can ever replace our Ursula, but at least it will keep you and me out of the kitchen."

34

Tennent did not let any grass grow under his feet. He called all the hospitals in the Los Angeles area to inquire about Ms. Penny Wells. Once he found where she had been hospitalized, he called to ask for the nurses' station.

"I'm Ms. Well's cousin. I'm calling to find out her condition."

"Resting comfortably." The nurse on duty reported.

"Can she have visitors?"

"Not at the present time."

"Thanks for your help, nurse, and the information."

"You're welcome, sir." She began to ask the caller's name, but Tennent had already hung up the phone.

He stewed with anger for not killing her when he had the chance and vowed to make things right. *She ain't gonna put a hole in my boat.*

He checked out of his hotel and went to the airport.

"I must get to Long Beach, California, as soon as possible. When is your next flight?" He asked the ticket agent.

"I can put you on a flight in about two hours. Shall I book you, sir?"

Once landing in Long Beach, he retrieved his luggage and went to the car rental counter. "Leonard Bertram here. I need to rent a car for a few weeks. I'll probably return it in another city if that's okay."

"Of course, sir." The young man behind the counter began filling out some papers.

"Here's my card," Tennent handed it over to the attentive clerk. He grabbed the morning newspaper from the counter, signed the rental agreement, took the keys, and went off to find his car.

His next stop was a café for breakfast and to read the newspaper and to think. *I've got to figure out a way to get into her room. Maybe an orderly would be a good idea. Could pose as a janitor even. There's always a room with supply scrubs and closets of cleaning supplies.*

Pleased with his new set of plans, he sat back in the booth savored his coffee and huevos rancheros.

Obsessed beyond reason, Tennent couldn't wait to end Penny's life, even if it meant losing his too.

Back in his rental car, Tennent pounded on the steering wheel. "I could have married Lavinia. I could be living the life of Riley in Monaco or some island in the south Pacific, but you had to put your foot in it. I'll give you your comeuppance, you snobby red-haired bitch." He continued with his epithets for a few minutes before he calmed down and began driving out to the freeway.

I can't stay in the San Fernando Valley. Too many prison buddies I don't want to see. I don't know much about the east side of the county. Maybe I should find a motel room near Pasadena, drive around, and learn the area. I'll have to have an escape route—good thinking there, Tennent.

Tennent found an obscure motel with a strange configuration. The parking lot went from one street through the property's backside and had an exit to another street. "Just what I need."

The clerk behind the desk greeted, "How may I help you, sir?"

"Good morning. I'm Leon Bertram. I'd like a room, please. By any chance, do you have one at the back of the motel? It should be quieter there."

"Of course, it is quieter, sir. Did you notice the

backside opens to a road to the cemetery?" The clerk quietly snickered at his joke.

"No, I didn't, but that's fine. I like quiet. Any places around here to grab a bite to eat? I'll probably be here for at least a week."

"Drive over to Rosemead Boulevard. That's to the east of us. You should find many places to eat. The Northwoods Inn is expensive, but good food, great steaks. And if you go toward Pasadena, Colorado Boulevard has some authentic Asian food. Sign the register, please. Here's your key. My name's Tombo. If you need anything, just call the office."

"Thanks for all your ideas, Tombo. Right now, I think I'm going to take a nap. I'm tired. I just flew in from Mexico, and it was a long flight." Tennent took the key, noticed it was room thirteen. "I've got to make that my lucky number."

Several hours later, Tennent woke and decided he should do a little casing of the hospital. He stopped at a florist, bought a plant, wrote a card, drove to the hospital, and went to the lobby's information desk.

"I have this plant to deliver to a Miss Penny Wells. Can you tell me what room?"

After a glance at the computer, the receptionist said, "Miss Wells is in ICU and cannot have visitors. You could leave the plant here or take it to the ICU nursing station."

"I'd rather take it to the station if it is permissible."

"Take the first bank of elevators to the third floor. Nurses station will be on your right as you exit the elevator."

"Thank you so much."

Tennent exited the elevator but didn't approach the nurse's station. Instead, he went in the opposite direction, peering into all the rooms. He rounded the corner and stopped dead in his tracks. Two police officers were standing outside a room. *That's got to be her room. Now to figure out a way to get inside.*

He continued his walk down the hallway, past the police, and rounded another corner. Walking a few more feet, he reached the nurses' station again. Putting on a smile, he approached the counter. "Hello, I have this plant to deliver to Miss Penny Wells."

"I'm sorry, sir, but no one is allowed in her room."

"Could I leave it here with you? I wanted to find out how my dear cousin is doing. Such a dreadful thing to happen to her."

"Yes, it was. And so senseless. Ms. Wells does so much for the community."

"Will she recover?"

"We know she has the will to fight. She'll survive, I'm quite certain. Do you want to leave your name and a message?"

"There's a message on the card," Tennent said as he skittered toward the open elevator. *Now would be the time to explore the hospital. It's late enough; there aren't too many people here.*

He surveyed the first floor, hopped into another elevator and pushed the call button for one of the lowest levels.

He stepped out into a supply floor. *Maybe I can find some scrubs, a mask, and some janitorial clothes.* Tennent discovered an unalarmed exit door at the end of a long narrow hallway that was lined with carts stacked with linens and medical supplies. *Good escape route. I'll have to see where this leads outside so I can park nearby.* He placed a box to hold the door ajar and walked out into the night air. *Where the hell am I? On another side street. This place is huge.*

He went back inside and searched for useful supplies, filling an empty bag with all his findings. His next stop was one floor lower to another sub-basement, where he discovered the janitorial supplies. "Jackpot," he said aloud.

Tennent found a restroom with lockers, most of them wide open. He walked around to see if there was an entrance to the outside. Another door led to a small courtyard with tables and benches. *When I get back to the motel, I'll try on my disguise. Now I think I'll find myself a nice dinner.*

The next day Tennent thought and thought about what he would do. He decided he would need a small-caliber gun with a silencer or a compact knife. He knew he had to do the deed in the next day or so because if Penny recovered, getting to her on the outside would be more difficult.

35

Jean-Luc managed to see a partner in Tom's firm.

"I can understand her reluctance in wanting to continue with Tom. If she would be agreeable, I'd be happy to be the new attorney of record."

"I think Lynn would be pleased. Do you think it would be possible to hold meetings here in Laguna so she wouldn't have to drive to your Pasadena office?"

"I see no problem with that. It will let me begin my weekend sooner. I know my wife will be thrilled."

"Will Lynn need to sign any papers? She'll be leaving for Atlanta next Wednesday, and she'll be gone for three days. She has a concert there."

"You are a good friend to her, Jean-Luc. Give her my card. I'll have the papers drawn up and ready to sign when she returns. May I drop them off at Hilltop?"

"Of course, just let Trudy know you are coming. With no Ursula, she is not as organized as she once was."

"Oh, my, that's right. Ursula was the woman found

murdered in the apartment downtown. Did they ever catch the person who did it?"

"Yes, he's in jail awaiting trial, but the mastermind is still on the loose. He thought he killed Penny Wells, but she survived, thank God. She will spend months recuperating. When she is released from the hospital, Trudy plans to have her at Hilltop to care for her. She'll hire a nurse and get whatever else might be needed. Trudy is also looking for a full-time housekeeper, cook, and personal assistant. Do you think your wife could recommend someone?"

"I will ask her."

Bright and early on Monday morning, Lynn called the law firm. "Mr. David Harrison, please. Mr. Harrison, this is Aisalynn Sheperd."

"Please call me David, if I may call you Lynn."

"Please do so."

"Lynn, Jean-Luc told me about your situation. We're neighbors in Laguna. I'm down there almost every weekend, so you would never have to come into the office and run into Tom. That would be most uncomfortable for you."

"That is very considerate, David. I leave for Atlanta on Wednesday morning, and I'll return on Sunday evening. Is there anything you need me to sign to change attorneys?"

"Just a formality. But you can do that when you return. I'll stay down on Monday so we can discuss your inheritance. If you want Jean-Luc or Trudy King there, that's fine with me."

"Since we don't have a cook anymore, do you think we could meet someplace for breakfast or coffee?"

"How about the Laguna Coffee Company? We can sit outside and probably stay longer than some of the other outdoor cafes."

"That sounds perfect. I'll see you on Monday morning."

Lynn, in need of a vehicle, loved the new car she chose with Jean-Luc. They thought it was ordinary enough that potential car thieves would leave it alone when parked at the airport. "It's terrible when I have to think of possibilities like that when buying a car. I'd like to have a bright red one! Oh well, one of these days, don't you think so, Jean-Luc?"

"I hope so. But this one has a sizable trunk; you can stuff a lot in it." He laughed. " Isn't that what all young ladies do?"

Lynn laughed with him. "I guess so. On a more somber note, Trudy called the hospital yesterday. Penny is not doing as well as expected. Trudy will stay in Penny's condo in Pasadena for several days, taking Chouchen with her. She hopes the dog might give Penny some extra incentive to rally."

"That's a great idea. Call the police department and let them know that no one will be on the premises for a few days. I know they've been diligent in looking for Tennent, but he seems to have vanished into thin air."

"Either Trudy or I will. We've had an ad in the paper for a Mary Poppins. But so far, no one even comes close to that description. Ursula is irreplaceable. I cry every time I think about her. Such a dear sweet person to come to such a horrible end."

36

Lynn fell in love with Atlanta once the taxi drove her down the tree-lined streets, under the shady canopy of lush, green leaves. She loved the soft scent of magnolia in the air. When she arrived at the hotel, she asked the front desk for a corner room so she could practice without disturbing the other guests.

Lynn played brilliantly, according to the Maestro and the newspapers' reviews. On her own, it was exciting to be in another state, performing in the open air before a sold-out crowd. The Maestro greeted her warmly and presented her with a list of upcoming concert dates, all in Europe. She had to sit down to read the agenda. "Maestro, are you certain I'm ready to do this? The number of concerts is overwhelming. How much new music will I have to learn?"

"Aisalynn, you can do anything. You probably have all the concertos in your repertoire now. It doesn't mean you will have to learn a new one for each city. You will be playing the same program repeatedly. You are the most wonderful thing to happen to the music scene in a long time. In my years of concertizing, I discovered it is necessary to have an assistant accompany you. There are too many details for you to contend with on your own. Is there someone you can ask to go with you?"

"I have two women in mind. Let me ask Trudy when I return to Laguna on Sunday. If neither one is available, I'll let you know right away."

Trudy waited anxiously for Lynn's return. She could not wait to hear all about the concert and tell her the good news about Penny.

Responding with such positivity during the visit with her dog, Chouchen, the doctors said Penny could go home within a week, maybe ten days. She could travel by car to Laguna. Trudy was pleased with that decision because an ambulance might draw attention and she didn't want Tennent seeing the emergency vehicle if he was scoping out the vicinity.

37

Tennent used the employee's entrance to the basement and put on the janitorial uniform. He casually pushed a supply cart to the Intensive Care Unit and passed Penny's room. Through the window, she could be seen propped up in bed. She looked a lot healthier than when he had last seen her, and most of the tubes were removed. *She's got to be dead yesterday.*

He pretended to study a clipboard and mentioned to the two sleepy police officers posted outside her door, "I need to clean this room."

"Okay, I'll accompany you. What's your name?"

"Leon."

"Well, be quick as you can, Leon." The police officer opened the door and ushered Tennent inside. The disguised janitor went through the motions, mopped the floors, and emptied the baskets. When he was done, he casually walked out. "I'll be back tomorrow night about the same time."

Once the custodian left, the police officer placed a call to Harley. "Boss, the victim just had a midnight visitor who claimed he was the janitor. I'm thinking that's not the janitor because a woman was here two hours ago giving the room a good cleaning."

"Did he give you any name?"

"Said it was Leon."

"Good work. If he is planning on a return visit, I think we'll have some plainclothes operatives waiting in the corridor. We won't let him get away."

38

"Tombo, when you get off work, come over to my room and have a beer with me. I want to talk with you."

"Sure thing, Mr. Leon."

Tennent opened a beer and set it in front of Tombo. He opened one for himself, taking a large swig.

"I'll come right to the point, my man. How would you like to earn some extra cash?"

"Always like to have more green in my pocket, but I ain't doin' nothin' illegal, am I? My parole officer had a hard enough time finding me this job, and I don't want to lose it."

"What were you in for?"

"B and E and assault. I was in Tehachapi for three years."

"I don't want to get you sent back. I only want you to drive a car for me. Pick me up at the hospital in Pasadena a little after midnight tomorrow night. If I get into any trouble, you just drive the car back here to the motel. I'll pay you $500 for your services."

"Do you want me to take you there too?"

"Not where you're going to pick me up. I'll show you so you can get familiar with the surroundings. We'll leave here a little after 11:00. You'll be off work by then." Tennent went over to the dresser, picked up his wallet and handed five crisp one hundred dollar bills to Tombo.

His eyes lit up. "Thanks, Mr. Leon. I'll see you tomorrow night."

The next evening, Tennent dressed in a suit and tie and waited for Tombo to arrive. A switchblade was tucked in his pocket and a gun in his ankle holster. The two drove to the street beside the employee entrance where Tennent wanted Tombo to wait. Then he had the young driver go around to the main entrance.

The guard checking guest identifications wasn't stationed at the desk, just inside the automatic doors.

Tennent walked right into the lobby, took an elevator to the housekeeping department in the sub-basement, put on the janitor's clothes, grabbed a rolling supply cart and then took the elevator to the third floor.

The police, anticipating a move by him, transferred Penny to a different room on another floor.

There was an undercover officer in her ICU bed, and guards flanked the door. Guards were also stationed outside the room where Penny was hidden.

Tennent walked into the ICU unit. "Hi guys, I'm here to clean the room."

Not able to move more than a few feet in either direction, the police ordered him to put up his hands.

"What the hell have I done? I am only doing my job, officer."

"William Tennent, you're under arrest for conspiracy to commit murder on one Ursula Becker and for aggravated assault and attempted murder on Penny Wells."

"My name is Leon Bertram. And I don't have the slightest idea who you are talking about." Tennent was not fast enough to grab his knife before one of the officers had his hands cuffed and behind his back.

"We'll see," said the other officer, "when we get you to the station."

They searched him and found the blade, went over his legs and found the gun. One of the officers noticed the clothes beneath the janitorial outfit. They had to cut off the uniform because they did not want to remove the restraints. Leg irons were secured to keep him from running.

Tombo, waiting outside when he saw the police lead Mr. Leon to a patrol car, drove back to the motel.

After reading about the capture in the newspaper the following morning, the motel clerk called the Pasadena Police Department.

Tombo figured it must be Mr. Leon they captured, even though he was identified as William Tennent. *I need to find out where they've got him locked up. His room will need to be cleaned for the next guest.*

"Pasadena Police Department. How may I direct your call?"

"Hello, I'm the desk clerk at the San Gabriel Motel. According to the newspaper, I believe you have arrested one of our guests. I need to find out where he is because his belongings are in his room. Will he be coming back here soon?"

"The man I think you are speaking about was taken to L.A. County jail. I can give you the phone number if you would like it."

Tombo took the number and called the arresting detective.

"I don't think he will ever be coming back. He's a career criminal and has been charged with several felonies."

"Wow, should I bring his belongings to you? Or would someone come here and get them? I need to have the housekeeper clean the room. Mr. Leon was due to check out today."

"That's not his real name. It's William Tennent, and he is one very bad apple. I will send someone to pick up his belongings. Just keep them at the front desk for me."

"He has a car here. What shall I do with it?"

"Don't worry. We'll have someone take care of that too."

Tombo hung up before the detective could ask his name.

39

Penny was scheduled for release from the hospital in the next day or so. Trudy spoke with the doctor. "I would like to bring her to my home in Laguna. The weather here is ideal for recovery. Penny can sit out on the deck and enjoy the sunshine and the ocean."

"Sounds wonderful. Can I come too?" The doctor teased.

"Is Penny able to sit comfortably for the two-hour drive? I can order a limousine so a nurse could accompany her."

"I believe that would be acceptable."

"When can I expect her?"

"How about Thursday, mid-afternoon? Ms. Wells will be released after lunch."

"Wonderful! Thank you, doctor." One could hear the smile on Trudy's lips. "Her room, her bed, and her beloved dog will be waiting for her. I need to engage a full-time nurse. Is there any registry you recommend?"

"The nurse accompanying Penny may be interested in taking care of her. Do you have another bedroom where she could stay?"

"Yes, I do. The nurse will enjoy the accommodations here. Please do call me as soon as you know."

Julie Appleton was thrilled to get the position. It turned out she would be the Mary Poppins Trudy and Lynn had been wanting. Besides her nursing skills, she was a whiz in the kitchen. Julie could not believe the state-of-art kitchen Ursula cooked in and reigned over. Although Julie's food differed from Ursula's, she cooked the same menu and no one complained. Trudy thought Julie was a godsend.

Trudy bought Penny a wheelchair, and Julie was able to take her out to the terrace where she could dine, read, or watch the waves crashing against the shoreline. Chouchen remained by her side day and night.

"Julie," Trudy asked. "I'm not certain what to offer as your monthly salary. What are you getting paid for nursing? What was your salary for cooking and housekeeping? Did you have a live-in arrangement before, or were you paying rent?"

Julie wrote down all the figures and detailed the work she had done previously. The two came to an agreement, and Julie was quick to accept her new position.

"Julie, the first order of business: we don't stand on ceremony here. I'm Trudy. You know Penny. Aisalynn, we call her Lynn, will be returning shortly. She had a performance in Atlanta this weekend. I don't know if Penny said anything to you, but I have a true concert violinist living with me.

"Next, we need to get your car here so you can shop and have a little bit of freedom on your time off. You're going to need house keys and the new codes for opening the gates."

"I thought I might take Sunday off and ride the train into L.A. Then I can take the metro into Pasadena, pick up my car and be back Monday morning. Does that work for you?"

"That will be splendid," said Trudy.

"My daughter lives in the apartment I'd been renting. I think she is planning to stay there. She's between jobs right now."

"How old is she?" Trudy's wheels are spinning. *Maybe she could go with Lynn as her companion.*

"She's almost 30."

"Please invite her back with you. We are looking for someone to be Lynn's personal assistant. Lynn will be performing all over Europe, so she will need someone to keep her organized. It would be a busy, exciting, and hectic job for anyone who does it."

"Oh my, I think I will call Heather right now."

Julie's daughter thought the job offer sounded exciting and challenging. She was a perfectionist and hoped Lynn would like her and hire her. She couldn't wait for her mother to arrive on Sunday.

Lynn arrived back at Hilltop, tired but still living on adrenaline. She was surprised to find Penny propped in bed in Ernst's old room.

"It's so good to be home. Even though I was only gone three days, I missed everyone." She patted the dog's head, "I missed you too! I hope I can become acclimated to playing twenty concerts. That is what I know of so far. They might add performances as we go along. I've got to find someone to help me. Trudy, would you help me write an ad?"

"Honey, I don't think that will be necessary. While

you were in Atlanta, Penny's nurse from the hospital, Julie Appleton, came here to care for her. She is also a professionally trained chef. Can you believe that? We have our Mary Poppins! Her daughter, Heather, has worked as an administrative assistant for ten years. She left the corporate world and wants to work in the private sector. If the interview goes well, you should hire her as your assistant. She can stay in the small guest room with the adjoining bath. Julie is comfortable in Ursula's old rooms. Wait until you sample her cooking."

"Things do work out eventually, don't they, Trudy? I guess you could say we've been fortunate, all things considered."

"You are so right. Are you too tired to have Jean-Luc here for dinner with us?"

"Never would I not want him here. He's been my lifesaver and my rock when it comes to Tom and all that went on. I do have a meeting tomorrow morning at nine with my new lawyer. I don't think I have any energy left to practice today. Think I'll visit with Penny and then take a nap."

"She will love having your company too. I'll have Julie bring refreshments, and we all can sit on the terrace while it's still warm enough for Penny. Then you can take your nap. We'll plan on cocktails tonight around 6:30. I'll call Jean-Luc and tell him what time."

Penny, Trudy, Jean-Luc, and Lynn sipped chilled white wine while Julie served a red potato salad with grilled wild salmon. The simple summer dinner ended with a fresh fruit sundae.

Penny's spirits were high, grateful to be alive and among friends. As soon as she felt physically able, she wanted to return to her home in Pasadena and get back to curating at the museum. She looked forward to mounting the exhibit from their trip to Germany. She needed to speak with the police regarding keeping a bodyguard. Would she need a chauffeur? Would she be able to drive? She knew she would be staying with Trudy for at least a month. Vinnie and Michel lived on Harbor Isle, not too many miles away, and she would love to have visits with them. She hadn't heard from the detectives. Did they catch the man that stabbed her? Was it Tennent?

40

Heather sat in the kitchen visiting with her mother. After dinner, everyone convened in the living room, where they planned to interview Heather. Lynn hoped it would go well. Being interviewed by a group of strangers at once might be daunting.

Heather proved to be a hit. A charming, well-spoken, and well-educated young woman, she and Lynn seemed to get along very well. "Do you think you might like a job of this nature? It won't be an easy one. I can be a bear at times."

"I've never been to Europe before," said Heather. "Do you think there will be any time for sightseeing?"

"I hope so," said Lynn. "I've never been to any of these cities. We could plan to see the sights together. If you would like the position, it's yours." Lynn stood up. "We will figure out a fair stipend for you, but you will have your plane tickets, accommodations, food, and anything related to taking care of me all paid for."

"I'd absolutely adore the job, Lynn. It sounds so exciting, even if it will be a lot of hard work. I am used to hard work."

"Then the first order of business is to apply for a passport for you. I leave for London in six weeks. I hope that will be enough time for you to get all the necessary paperwork done."

"I'll be happy to help with that," Jean-Luc said, "but it is getting late and I have a business appointment early in the morning. Thank you for the lovely dinner and the good conversation. It was a pleasure to meet you, Heather, and Julie. I'll see my way out." He blew kisses to everyone as he left.

On Tuesday morning, Penny made a phone call to Harley Bronson at the Los Angeles Police Department. "Mr. Bronson, Penny Wells, good morning."

"That's a nice voice to greet me this morning. I was going to call you."

"I want to know if you found the man who stabbed me."

"Yes, we did, just a couple of nights ago. Right

now, he is sitting in county jail waiting to be arraigned."

"That is great news! Was it Bill Tennent?"

"Affirmative. And we caught his accomplice in the Ms. Becker murder."

"Can you come to the house and tell me all about it? I'm recovering at Trudy King's house at Hilltop in Laguna."

"I'll make arrangements with Max Dedham in Laguna. Will Thursday around eleven in the morning work for you?"

"Perfect. I'll ask the cook to prepare sandwiches and iced tea, so bring your appetite. We can sit on the terrace and talk."

"See you then, Ms. Wells."

Penny felt her energy changing and attributed her new sense of well-being to the detective's positive conversation.

41

Julie helped Penny zip her pale green summer dress. She looked at herself in the mirror and could see her red hair tinged with silver. *Not too worse for wear.* She looked again in the mirror and added a summery pink color to her lips.

Trudy knocked and walked in. "You look marvelous, Penny. I'm so glad. I haven't seen you looking so well since we were in Berlin."

"Julie, you truly have been a godsend to Penny. Well, to all of us. The doctor was so right in recommending you. I don't think you'll devote much more time to nursing duties, but we will certainly be looking forward to all your fine cooking. I think the Appleton ladies will be around for many years to come."

Effusive from Trudy's praise, Julie blushed. "Thank you, Trudy, and thank you, Penny. It's been wonderful to see you spring back to life. We weren't so sure a few weeks ago; it was touch-and-go for a bit."

Come Thursday morning, the two detectives arrived and were escorted to the terrace.

"May I join you?"

"Of course, Mrs. King," said Harley. "Then we won't have to repeat ourselves." The detective glanced at notes in his spiral-bound pad. "Let's bring you up to date with what we discovered during the investigation.

"Penny, once Tennent left you for dead, he changed his appearance. He gave his car to a friend, the one who murdered Ms. Becker. He went to a bar near his apartment, spun a tale of how he had to get back to Chicago. The bartender helped him get a cab to the Burbank airport.

"From what we can determine, he stayed at this hotel in Chicago and bought another wardrobe, changing his appearance again.

"We learned he was planning to fly to Mexico City and had someone forge a new passport. We know he never left the country because he read in the Chicago paper that you were not dead.

"He scrapped his plans and took a return flight to Long Beach. With the newly forged documents, he rented a car under his assumed name.

"From there, he went to a motel in San Gabriel and rented a room for a week. He went to the hospital, learned all the exits and where the janitorial supplies were kept. He put on janitorial clothes and took the supply cart to your room in the ICU.

"You had been under police protection around-the-clock. The officers on duty realized something was unusual because the room had been cleaned two hours earlier when he showed up.

"The next time Tennent came, we were ready for him. You had been moved to another room, and an undercover officer was in bed in your old room in the ICU.

"Luckily, there was no gunfire. He had a gun in an ankle holster and a switchblade in his pocket. He surrendered, but not too quietly. It was quite a scuffle. He insisted we got the wrong person.

"He enlisted the help of the hotel clerk; the unsuspecting fellow was on probation. I believe he was manipulated and acted unwittingly. I hope he doesn't lose his job and be sent back to prison. He's been cooperative with us."

"But if Tennent didn't murder Ursula, how did you find out?" Penny and Trudy were most interested in the latest developments.

"Strangely enough," said Max, "it was through your friend, Dr. Lottie Wasserman."

"How did she get involved?" Trudy asked.

"A man named Payton from the Beverly Hills Art Galleries called her and asked if she wanted to buy a Driscoll painting. Dr. Wasserman made an appointment for him to come by on a Sunday afternoon. When she saw the painting, she knew it was yours and where it had hung in your home.

"Payton was abashed and said he had no idea the painting had been stolen. Dr. Wasserman told us he began perspiring and dabbed his forehead with a handkerchief. She realized he was innocent, duped.

"The doctor and the gallery owner called my office, and we divulged a plan to capture Tennent. Payton was told to delay the Driscoll sale, saying Dr. Wasserman had to sell some stock and wait for the settlement. Before he got the money, Tennent gave his accomplice $5,000, telling him he scored a great deal for $10,000."

"That scoundrel even double-crosses his friends, doesn't he? Well, I'm glad he's behind bars. Will I have to testify? Will Penny have to testify?"

"I don't believe so, Trudy. The D.A. hasn't said yet, but you will have to stick around in case we need you."

"I'm so glad he's been caught." Relieved, Penny was all smiles. "Now I can go back to work at the museum. I want to see the results of what we found in Berlin."

"Ms. Wells, please don't try to tackle anything until your doctor gives you full clearance. You have been under someone's care since you arrived in Laguna. That's not the same as being on your own. I think you should wait until you have been back in Pasadena for a few weeks. I also want to see you have twenty-four-hour protection and a chauffeur. Our two police departments want to leave nothing to chance."

"I can live with that. Living at Trudy's is like a vacation."

"I can see why," said Harley Bronson. "This is one of the most beautiful places I've ever been."

"My father, Peter Wells, was an architect. This was the last piece of property he designed before he passed away." Penny told him. She was proud of her father's accomplishments.

"He did a fantastic job. Was he the same Peter Wells who was one of the first American spies during World War Two?"

"Yes, he was," said Penny, appreciative of Harley's comments.

"I just read a great article on him. I love history and war stories."

"Then you may be interested in what we are doing. Lynn inherited an estate, contents included, in East Berlin. I would call it a castle. In July, we went to pack up everything we could find. There were many hidden compartments throughout, and we had to cut into walls and floors to retrieve priceless treasures. What we came up with was amazing, pieces of history. Everything was shipped to the Los Angeles County Museum of Art before we returned.

"I am going to curate the entire group of paintings, whatever other interesting artifacts, and we will hopefully have the stories to go along with it. One of the most exciting pieces we found was a priceless Guarneri violin. Lynn is using it to practice. She is an incredible violinist and will be setting out on a world tour within the month."

"What a dynamic household you have here, Mrs. King. And Ms. Wells, as a history buff, I would be most interested in what you are doing. Here are a few of my cards; let's stay in contact."

Julie made her entrance to clear the table and offer more refreshments. Harley stared, interested in the woman with the large brown eyes and silky long brown hair. They exchanged a brief awkward smile.

"Julie is my new house manager and personal chef. She is Ursula's replacement, although Ursula could never be replaced. Julie is a blessing to me." Trudy could not utter enough kind words about the new caretaker.

"I'm Harley Bronson. It's a pleasure to meet you, Julie. Mrs. King, you are a fortunate lady."

"Yes, I'm well aware of that fact. Julie is a nurse and came here to care for Penny. Now she wears more than one hat. Her daughter, Heather, is Lynn's personal assistant. The Maestro suggested Lynn brought someone with her when she travels to Europe. He certainly didn't want her traveling alone."

"That's a great thing. How is she doing after that knife attack? She was fortunate that the blade didn't get any closer. We know that knife was meant for Ms. Wells. She was standing right next to Lynn when that homeless man slashed her. We will charge Tennent for a felony on that count. Even if we never find the man who did the actual stabbing, the D.A. said he could prove it on a conspiracy. I want this guy in jail for the rest of his life. Throw away the key." Harley was vehement in his pronouncement.

Max motioned to Harley. "I think we should take our leave. You have a long drive back to L.A., and we have been here a lot longer than expected. It was like a day off, though."

"Yes, it was. And we both enjoyed ourselves, even though we came on business. Lunch was great, especially the charming company."

On the way to their cars, Max gave Harley a playful punch in the arm. "Are you talking about the people or Julie in particular? I saw your eyes wandering."

Harley opened the car door of his sedan and climbed in. He felt happier than he had in years. "That Julie, what a beautiful smile. I've got to know her better."

42

"Heather, we need to get the paperwork and apply for your passport today, also take the concert list and find out which countries will require a visa. I hope you like shopping because that's what we're going to do after the passport business is addressed."

"Whatever you say, Lynn. I just don't want you to be too tired and especially since you are still recovering from your wound."

"Don't worry; I'll be just fine. We don't have to leave Laguna today. Most of the things I want are here in town, or we can go over to Fashion Island in Newport. That's not too far away."

One of the first stores they visited sold musical instruments and supplies. "I will always need a good supply of strings in case one breaks during a concert or practice. I expect you to keep me with a good stock all the time." Lynn looked at Heather.

"Does that actually happen?"

"Isaac Stern had one break during his concert at Davies Hall. That was many years ago. But if it could happen to him, it could happen to me."

"How many do you want me to keep on hand?"

"Five should do nicely," said Lynn. "Also rosin and a couple of very soft cloths, like this one." Lynn held the material up for her assistant to feel.

Heather made a note of Lynn's request, took a business card from the store proprietor. She would call him later and set up an account. Next, Lynn wanted to visit a luggage store. Heather thought she checked out every piece of luggage in the store before deciding which set to purchase. Heather couldn't believe the high price tag on the set Lynn chose.

"Heather, find a set of luggage for yourself," said Lynn. "We need to look very smart."

Heather chose a conservative set of lightweight luggage she knew would be easy to carry.

Lynn told the clerk she wanted everything delivered to Hilltop.

"I'm famished, Heather. How about you?"

"I can always eat. Where do you want to go?"

"Someplace that has decent chicken salad

sandwiches. I love them. And your mom will be fixing dinner for everyone tonight, so I don't want to spoil my appetite."

Not more than a half-hour later, the two ladies were blissfully munching on their sandwiches and drinking Arnold Palmers, laughing together with small talk.

"I want to look at the evening gowns at Nordy's. I don't need to take many dresses, but I would like a couple to switch off from concert to concert. You have a great style sense, and I can use your input."

"I appreciate the compliment. Do you want something custom made or off the rack?"

"I really don't care, as long as it is pretty, easy to wear, and easy to move my arms."

"Let's go and see what we can find. You said we would be leaving for New York in two weeks. Do you want to shop there too?"

"No time. I'll be practicing and practicing for the concert at Carnegie Hall. Then there will be rehearsals and then the big night."

"It sounds fascinating. I'm thrilled to be part of it."

"It is, and I'm glad you'll be with me. This is my

first big concert since Davies Hall. I was scared to death with the huge responsibility. Being stabbed afterward was frightening. I feel jittery every time I think about it."

"I can't even imagine. The police said you were fortunate you weren't killed."

One of the clerks met Lynn and Heather in the evening gown department.

"Hello, I'm Aisalynn Sheperd." Heather thought the violinist sounded a little imperious but surmised this assistant role was new to her, and there was much to learn.

"You're the violinist I have been reading so much about. I'm so pleased to meet you. How may I be of help?"

Heather thought Lynn preened as she walked over to a comfortable couch and sat down. "I need two or three long dresses. I'm leaving in ten days to begin a lengthy concert tour, so I don't know if I have time for a custom gown or if I should buy off the rack."

"Let me show you what I have available."

"Heather, come and sit next to me. You're a part of this too."

Heather looked at the dresses the sales clerk brought out to show them, inwardly drooling at their beauty.

"No, this one won't do," said Lynn. "I can't have all this frou-frou. My arms need free movement. I don't like all the beading on this one. I like simple, tailored lines. No black, no white, no brown. I already have a gray dress. I like the green one. Let me try it on, please."

"That's a good color on you," Heather said as Lynn walked from the dressing room and twirled before the mirrors to check herself out.

"I want to try that royal blue one." Lynn was pleased with the way the blue dress fit her. "I'll take this one too. Do you have anything else you can show me?"

"I have a satin dress in ice-blue and a silk taffeta in navy. I'll bring them both out now."

The navy dress was not full length. "Try that one on Heather. You're going to need clothes also."

"It's lovely, Lynn."

"And you look lovely in it too. It's yours. Now you find some others, and I will find one more dress. I don't care for the satin one. We can leave here and go to Saks."

Heather watched Lynn hand the clerk her credit card and instructed her to send the clothes to Hilltop.

"Heather, I want you to wear black, navy, or gray at all times when you're with me so we will look professional in all we do. I don't mean when we're sightseeing, just when we are dealing with concert stuff."

"I can do that, Lynn." Aghast at the money Lynn was spending, she could say nothing more.

Lynn could see how much Heather liked some dresses on the mannequin in the next store window. They walked into the store and ordered three new dresses to be sent to Hilltop. "Lynn, that's enough. I don't even know where I'll put them."

"You'll find a place, trust me. If they don't fit or look right, we'll send them back. Let's try that boutique over there." She spotted a teal silk crepe with an attractive drape. "I like those dress lines. Think I could play easily with it." She tried it on, bought it, and had it sent along with everything else to Hilltop.

"Lynn, we should go back to Laguna. You need to have some rest."

"I am getting a little tired. Would you like to drive home?"

Trudy greeted the girls at the door, anxious to see all the purchases.

"They will be delivered tomorrow, Trudy, at least that is what the stores promised. We will give you a fashion show. I want to lie down for a couple of hours. Don't let me sleep too long."

Heather went to see her mother in the kitchen. "Mom, can you sit and talk with me?" Heather sat down at the cozy kitchen nook. "I can't believe all the money Lynn spent on me today! It was crazy!" The daughter leaned in to whisper to her mother. "She bought me four dresses; the total cost was over $1000. She also bought me a $700 set of luggage. She bought dresses for her concerts. I know they must have cost over $1000 apiece. I've never seen anyone spend like that. Am I working for a diva? And we applied for my passport."

"Sounds like you had a wonderful time. Lynn is an extremely wealthy young woman. She inherited an incredible sum from her great uncle. I'm sure spending money is new to her; she might be going a bit overboard."

"Do you want some help with dinner?"

"No, sweetheart, everything is all set. I need to help Penny find a bodyguard who can also help with nursing and cooking. She can hire a housekeeper for the rest. I thought I'd talk to that detective Harley to see if he can recommend someone."

"Mom, is that just an excuse so you can talk to him. Do you like him?"

Julie smiled without reply.

"You are smitten! I'm glad for you, Mom."

43

A cursing yell pierced the atmosphere. The quiet buzzing of the police department was now filled with shouting. "How in the hell did he do it?"

Detective Bronson had been sitting at his desk catching up on an old file. He had just hung up from a call with Julie. Harley hoped to have a date with her soon. *Such a nice lady, good looking too.*

An officer stuck his head into Harley's cubicle. "Tennent escaped out of the transport van."

"WHAT?" was the first thing Harley could say. "When? Does anyone know how?"

"They were transporting him from an overflow jail to here. He jumped out of a moving van into the side brush of the freeway."

"Get out an APB immediately. I've got to call Max and tell him."

Harley was gritting and gnashing his teeth when he got on the line with Max.

"How in the hell did it happen? Those chains and locks are supposed to be escape-proof." Max was fuming.

"God only knows how he got out of them."

"He has a lot of prison pals who are out of now. I'm sure he's going to find one to help him. I don't think it will be Deke. He's been staying away from Tennent and keeping his hands clean. His parole officer said he couldn't believe the change in him."

"Good for Deke. What about Tony Fazio?"

"Heard he was just released. I'm sure the news made its way to Tennent in his cell. That may be where he is headed."

"We should pay a visit to Fazio and see what's going on. We need to warn Tombo, too. He has been cooperative, and I don't want Tennent to be the reason he goes back to prison. The kid has cleaned up his act."

"Let's put some plainclothes out on the streets to find Fazio and any known associates. Even though it's been a few years, we ought to check on the whereabouts of the rest of the gang involved in the gallery heist."

Tennent busied himself getting rid of the orange jumpsuit with large white DOJ letters printed on the back. He had a great story to relate to whoever found him. "I was carjacked at gunpoint. The guy stole my clothes, my wallet, and the car. He has my driver's license."

Oh yes, and there would even be more of a story. "My name is Larry Benson. I'm here from Illinois. I'd just like to get to my friend's home in Los Angeles. Where am I now?"

The first person who saw Tennent standing at the side of the freeway in underwear came to his aid. "The stars are aligning to help you today, Billy boy," he whispered to himself. "He's a young kid, maybe twenty and out to do a good deed." He studied his rescuer.

"That's some set of wheels ya got there."

"Thanks," the good Samaritan replied. "I've been working on it for over three years. Parts are hard to come by when a car is this old. I'm entering it into a car show next month."

"What's your name, son?"

"Denny, sir. Dennis Watson."

"Well, Denny Watson, I appreciate your help, and if you give me your address, I will see you are compensated for all your trouble." Tennent poured out all the old charm.

"I don't want the money, sir. I'm happy to help. Just pay it forward to the next person you can help. That's what my mama taught me."

"Your mother sounds like one smart lady."

Tennent asked Denny to borrow his cell phone. He called Big Tony and, without revealing his true identity to Denny, relayed information.

"Right now, I'm about an hour away from where you are. I'm not at home." Tony was acting cagey since he didn't want to reveal Tennent's identity. "Do you have any clothes, Larry?" He tried to pick a place that would draw no attention towards the two men quietly meeting.

"Only the skivvies the thief left on me."

"Let me talk to the person helping you."

"Denny, Larry and I are about the same size. I have plenty of clothes he can borrow. My apartment is hard to find, so listen up."

It wasn't too difficult for Denny to find the apartment. It was less than thirty minutes from where he found Tennent on the side of the freeway. He stayed with him until Big Tony arrived so Larry wouldn't have to stand out in public without any clothes. Half an hour later, Tony drove up to meet them. They both thanked Denny, who still refused to accept any money.

"Thanks so much, pal. You're a real sport."

Tennent shook his hand. "Good luck in the car show. If I'm still here, I'd love to come and see it."

44

Back at the police station in Los Angeles, Harley whipped a wastebasket at the wall, the papers spilled to the floor. "You idiots! How in the hell can you lose a prisoner?"

The two transport officers took the berating. "It just happened. The chains and cuffs were secure."

"He got out of them. That's all I can say," pleaded the other officer. "He didn't use a key. It was like a magic trick. Locked in one minute and freed the next."

Harley got back on the phone with Max to discuss the case in depth. "He has one objective, to kill Penny Wells. Get some protection to her house. I want a twenty-four-hour bodyguard service stat. I can send two women from this office. Do you have anyone from your division you can spare for at least two weeks, maybe more?"

Max laid out the protection details to the officers. "We need to devise a schedule so that Ms. Wells remains guarded at all times. Blend in. We want it to look like you're visiting Hilltop, not protecting its residents.

"This afternoon we will go to Hilltop so you can meet Ms. Wells and get familiar with the vicinity. She was kind enough to offer meals while on duty."

"That sounds like a nice perk," said the older policewoman.

"I guarantee when this duty is over, you probably won't want to leave. These folks are upstanding citizens, all-'round great folks. They do not deserve to live in fear of Tennent. Trudy King, the owner of Hilltop, has invited us over to meet everyone and to get the lay of the land."

The female officer said, "We will do all we can to serve and protect Ms. Wells and help you find Tennent. The first thing he will do is get his hands on a weapon. He's probably armed by now and more dangerous than ever."

"I know you are right. Let's get moving. It is time for us to be on our way to Hilltop. Did Harley say anything to you gals about staying in a motel instead of returning home each night?" Max asked the two officers from Laguna.

"No, he didn't, but it's fine by me," said the one

officer who lived in Laguna.

"No problem," said the other female officer. "Tell us which motel and we will be there."

Later that afternoon, the four female officers, the two detectives, and the friends of Hilltop were gathered on the terrace getting acquainted. Julie served iced tea and crispy, hot chicken wings with plenty of napkins.

"May I have your attention, please," Trudy said, interrupting the ongoing flow of conversation. "I'm so grateful to Max and Harley for arranging this charade. That's about all I can call it because you will not be appearing in your official capacity. We are very informal here, so please call us by our first names. I'm Trudy, and you have already met Penny. That charming gentleman with a French accent is Jean-Luc. Aisalynn, Lynn, as she prefers, is our resident virtuoso. Julie is our new chef du jour and does double-duty as Penny's nurse.

"When Penny is well enough to return home in Pasadena, you two ladies from Los Angeles will be assigned to protect her there. If that doesn't meet your schedule or you are reassigned, please let Harley know so you can be replaced. We want everything to run as smoothly as possible.

"If there is anything you can't eat, please let Julie know. The refrigerator is always open to you. Don't be shy about taking a snack. You'll find a coffee machine on the counter, coffee cups, and a selection of coffee and tea.

"In the den, you can watch the television, read books and magazines, or use the computer. Take a catnap if you like. Don't feel you have to sit and watch Penny every moment. We all watch her."

"This sounds more like a vacation than a job," said one of the female officers.

Trudy gave everyone a tour of the house, the grounds, and the gates. "Please ask if there is anything else you might need."

"I've got to head back. Thank you for your hospitality, Trudy." Max made the rounds shaking hands.

Harley did not want to leave just yet. *I'll have to ask Julie to make more of those wings for me. They were spicy, just the way I like them.* He squeezed Julie's hand on the way to the door.

Julie smiled and mouthed the words, "Talk to you later, Harley."

45

Larry Benson, formally known as Bill Tennent, woke
from his nap and looked around the room. "This place is a
roach coach, what a dump. I can't stay in this pigsty. I've
got to get some cleaning supplies. Since it is cheap and off
the beaten path, I don't expect the cops to come bang on
the door. When Tony arrives, I'll ask him to front me
some money. I blew through my stash and need to get
supplies and a change of clothes."

While Tennent was talking to himself, Tony
knocked on the door. "Hey Larry, are you hungry?"

"Silly question Tony, let's go eat."

"There's a hole in the wall diner a few doors from
here. Let's go there. The food can't be that bad. The joint
is always busy."

The two criminals walked down the street to The
Greasy Spoon. A help-wanted sign hung in the front
window.

"Larry, you should apply for the job. Maybe you would get a meal or two thrown in. That would help you, wouldn't it?"

"Yeah, but let's eat first. I'm starved. I'll have the Blue Plate special." He looked at the man behind the counter wearing a greasy apron.

"And your buddy?"

"I'll have the same."

"Tony, I need to borrow some money. That room is scuzzy, filthier than a prison. I need some Clorox, Comet, and rags. I'd also like to get some new sheets and a blanket. The ones on the bed look like they've never been washed."

"Sure, Larry, we will go right after we eat. These ribs are delicious. They fall right off the bone." Tony was smacking his lips and licking his fingers.

After Tony paid for their dinner, Larry asked the man behind the counter if the job was still available. "What are the hours? And what is the job?"

"It's the midnight to eight in the morning shift, dishwasher, coffee maker, and serve at the counter if needed."

"I can do that."

"What's your name?"

"Larry Benson."

"Well, Larry, you're hired. You can start tomorrow night. I will pay you in cash each shift."

"Great, I'll be here at midnight. Thanks."

Tony and Tennent left the diner. "Did you hear that, Tony? He didn't even want any ID or social. That's a great break for me. Of course, he could get caught if the IRS knew he wasn't documenting his employees."

"Maybe they don't stick around very long."

"Well, whatever, I won't worry about it. Hey, I see a Kmart down the street, over there on the left."

It didn't take Tennent long to find the cleaning supplies, a new shower curtain, a bathmat, towels, a set of sheets, a warm blanket, and toiletries. "I think I have all I need right now, Tony. I will square up with you back as soon as I can. If I make $80 a shift, I'll have $80 to spend. And I get paid the next morning besides. I'll be fine."

"No problem, man. We need to lay low and can't be seen together every day."

"I figured that. You could come into the diner late at night or early in the morning, and we could talk."

"There's a lake with a walking path around it not

too far from here. We could meet at one of the benches and talk."

"Give me some exercise too. Good idea, Tony. Fresh air and fresh ideas to get rid of that glib bitch."

"Tennent, I would think you would want to give up your fixation on Ms. Wells. Don't you value your freedom more?"

"If they catch me before I accomplish my deed, I'll still be going to prison. It don't matter. I hate her guts, and I want her dead, dead, dead." Tennent emphasized the word dead louder and louder.

Each day, Tennent showed up for his job, collected his money, and went back to the motel to lay low. He found a place in his room where he could hide his daily pay. After a week, the money was adding up.

Planning his next move, Tennent decided it was time to change his appearance again. He grew a beard and dyed his hair. A new Dodgers cap helped him blend in with the crowd. When Tony saw him again, he barely recognized his friend.

"You look good, Bill. Even healthy."

"Feeling good. But I've come to the realization I can't buy a car because I have no identification. If I steal a car, it could be found before I make a getaway. What do you think about stealing a motorcycle?"

"It's great for a getaway, but where would you be going?" You would have to dump the bike, and then what?"

"I thought about ending up in the central valley, maybe Madera, Fresno somewhere like that."

"For how long? You are going to need enough money to get an ID and a social. I don't think you should plan to go to another country."

"Tony, you keep throwing up all these roadblocks."

"I know, but you are my friend. Just looking out for ya, bro."

"I shanked that bitch, and she survived. I'm gonna shut her up for good if it's the last thing I do."

"Do you want to spend the rest of your life in the slammer scrubbin' the johns and sweepin' 'n moppin' floors? Remember the time you got beat up in the yard and ended spending thirty days in the hole? Wouldn't you rather live in the free world?'

"Like I already said, not as much as I want her dead."

"Where is she now?"

"I'm not sure. But I know she can't be in Pasadena. I have a hunch she's in Laguna at her friends on the hill. From what I could see when I was in her hospital room, she has a long road to recovery ahead. She wasn't supposed to survive. After Bernie offed the housekeeper, I expect that house is locked up tighter than a drum, closely guarded too."

"There's got to be a way for you to get in."

"You need to get a new burner phone and ditch that phone you have in the ocean, so there's no trace of you or me talking with Denny, the kid who came to my rescue."

"Good point about the phone. I could get my girlfriend to deliver some flowers to the house. She could at least get inside the compound."

"Maybe. Let me think about that. For now, I gotta get my jam on and move again. We need to find me another place to stay that is off the beaten path."

Tony pulled into the parking lot of a nondescript motel on Los Angeles's outskirts, close to Glendale and the freeway.

"Can we get a room for a week? Two beds?" Tony asked the clerk.

The clerk looked at the two of them. "That'll be $150 upfront, cash. I don't take credit cards or checks."

Tennent ponied up the money in small bills.

"Thank you, gentlemen. Here's your key. I can give you two if you'd like. It's room seven."

"I've got to buy more clothes, Tony. I can't keep wearing your clothes, which swim on me, or go around in my undershorts."

"There's a thrift store down the street."

"That's perfect. I don't need nothin' fancy. I gotta get me some more peroxide or hair dye so I can keep my new look."

"Once we're done shopping, there's a pizzeria next to the motel. We can eat there unless you want to eat in your room."

"We can eat there, Tony. Think I'll take a short nap after we eat. Then we can put on our thinking caps and hatch a plan."

"If you need cash, I've been doing a little small-time dealing to make some extra money. Maybe you could do that. Cops aren't always looking over my shoulder."

"Maybe. I need to earn some cash for clothes and food and pay for this cockroach motel. I can still work at The Greasy Spoon. The owner is nice and he doesn't ask questions. It's a real come-down to the lifestyle I once had, but this is just temporary. It'll all change once I get rid of Penny Wells. That's a solemn oath."

46

As summer approached, Larry grew increasingly agitated at not finding Penny Wells. His entire being was in kill-mode. Patience was not his best virtue.

He read that the violinist would be playing at the Hollywood Bowl, and a new plan hatched. *That's an awful lot of people to make a getaway work. It would be easier to do it at the museum, not so many people around. I'll have to think about this for a few days. Maybe I could rig a bomb to her car. That's not my specialty, but I know Mad Dog has experience with explosive devices. She'd go out with a bang.* Tennent laughed. *Have to tell Tony my idea. Wow, it's brilliant.* But the idea was just that, an idea. It didn't go any farther than in Tennent's mind.

It had been almost a year since Penny survived the stabbing. She felt like her old self and was able to work regular hours at the museum. Even though she felt safe and well protected by the bodyguards protecting her, she worried Bill Tennent might find a way to hurt her again.

Penny, stop being paranoid. You are safe and in the hands of skilled bodyguards.

During Penny's recovery, the staff cataloged the Berlin shipment, and the exhibit was ready to be mounted. Due to the provenance of the art, Penny knew it would generate tremendous public interest.

Jean-Luc had suggested the museum nationally advertise the exhibit because it might be possible to return some pieces to the rightful heirs. Someone might even provide reclamation leads if one of their ancestors owned these paintings when the Nazis ransacked and pillaged the European countries they marched into and conquered.

Penny walked through the galleries, checking each submission and reading over each accompanying set of remarks to ensure the words matched the collection's proper piece. Everything looked perfect. The large-donor reception would be the following night, and she wanted no errors.

"I wish Ernst were here to guide us. Perhaps I can enlist Lottie. Since she lived through part of the war in Berlin, she might have some ideas to help people become reunited with their family's history. How lucky she was to have Ernst rescue her."

47

Tennent religiously read the daily paper to find snippets about Penny's latest activities. She was a favorite subject of the society page, and even though Tony teased him, he read every word.

"Hey, big guy, there's a huge to-do at the museum next Saturday night. Maybe that would be a good time to kill her?"

"Are you sure?" Tony was feeling uncomfortable.

"I think you're getting soft in your old age, man. I'm beginning to come alive."

Tony worried that Tennent's personality was changing, growing darker. He appeared driven in his scheming and didn't seem to remember a lot of current details. Mistakes were ripe for the making. All he talked about was killing Penny Wells. *I need to distance myself from Tennent. If he succeeds in what he's planning, I could be indicted too. Friend or not, I don't need that, and I ain't going back inside.*

After finishing his midnight shift at the diner, Tennent called Tony and asked him to meet him at the reservoir. It was an easy walk from the motel.

Tennent showed Tony a clipping from the newspaper. "Look, there's going to be a public showing of a new collection at the museum. This will be the time to do it. I feel it. I have my gun and ammo. Now all I need is a suit and tie to look presentable. Tony, take me to a store where I can buy a new outfit, not a second-hand shop or K Mart."

"Let's bounce and get you some new threads. You've been lucky to stay off the police radar for over a year. Maybe they've stopped looking."

"I doubt that."

Tony drove him to a discount men's store in a Los Angeles suburb. Tennent looked at the suits in his size and chose a stylish dark gray, almost black. He selected a pale gray shirt and a muted burgundy paisley tie. Tennent strutted in front of the mirror.

"I didn't recognize you. My god, you look so different."

"Think I'll fit in with the museum crowd?"

"I know you will. Just get a new haircut. It's beginning to look like you're wearing a mop. I'm kidding, of course, but a haircut would do wonders."

"Thanks, my friend. Now, if I can get you to drop me off a couple of blocks away from the museum on the gala night, I'll take it from there."

"I appreciate you not asking me to take part in your venture. I've no desire to go back to the joint. I'm seventy years old now."

"So am I, but I don't feel it, old man. Be ready for the finest performance of my life."

The next morning at shift change, Larry gave his boss a two-week notice.

"What are you going to do?"

Tennent, full of glibness, was quick to answer. "I discovered a relative I thought was dead. I'm going to Spokane, Washington, to stay with him for a month or two. I'm really looking forward to seeing him."

48

Tennent's big day came the following Saturday. He dressed with great care, making sure his shoes were shining, slicking down his new haircut as the barber had shown him. His beard was well-trimmed. Tennent looked at himself in the mirror and smiled at the results. "She'll never see me coming." He spun the cylinder to be sure his gun was fully loaded and tucked it inside the suit pocket.

At seven in the evening, Big Tony would be coming by. The plan was to drop Tennent off on Wilshire Boulevard, a short distance away from the Los Angeles County Museum of Art entrance.

"Yo, Tony, there's a florist up there on the right. Stop for a minute. I want to buy flowers. That will help get me up close and personal to Wells." He chose a bouquet of dark red funeral roses. "These should do the trick. I can hide the gun under the flowers. Thanks for driving me here Tony, you're a swell pal."

Tennent stepped out of Tony's car and onto the sidewalk. Exhilarated beyond belief, he made his way to the museum. When he entered the front door, he asked the guard where he might find Ms. Wells. "I've been told to give these to her personally. If I don't, my boss will have my head."

The guard laughed and pointed him to one of the galleries where drinks were being poured and canapés served. "Follow the music."

Tennent could hear musicians playing and admitted it did have a pleasing sound. *Nice for a murder.* He looked around the spacious gallery room. When Tennent saw Penny, he shook with excitement. *Bitch, you'll never leave this room alive.*

"Ms. Wells, you have destroyed my life!" He made certain everyone in the room could hear him, even with the music playing. "You accused me of stealing a painting once. You stuck your nose up at me wanting to date your cousin. I'm William Tennent, and you will be dead in the next one moment!"

Patrons began to scream and flee. Penny's loud scream was as vocal as all the women combined. The curator's reflexes were not fast enough to defend herself, and the female bodyguard moved quickly to protect her. Penny glared at the man who stood before her.

When the flowers dropped to the floor, it was then she saw the revolver in her nemesis's hand. "I want you dead!" he screamed at her, his red face suddenly turning white.

Tennent grabbed his chest. The career criminal fell where he stood, his gun skittered across the floor. His head bounced off the marble floor, and a halo of blood began to pool, the same color as the dark red roses around him. His face became ashen and clammy. A twitch and a gulp remained as his final movements.

A doctor, an art patron in attendance, parted the frantic crowd and bent over the body, checking for a pulse. He told the officer holding back the onlookers that it appeared he died of a massive coronary.

Harley Bronson, also in attendance at the gala, accompanied Julie. He couldn't believe it when he saw Tennent's lifeless body splayed on the floor. He called Max to let him know the news. "I wanted that bastard sent away for life. That miserable piece of shit got the easy way out."

"Are you okay? Jean-Luc led Penny to her office.

"Yes, I am. I am shaken up. When I saw that gun in Tennent's hand, everything moved in slow motion. I heard his head crack on the floor, even over all the noise. I thought I was going to die. I cannot believe it is over. Finally over after all these years. Once my legs stop trembling, we should go back out so I can address the crowd. Then we can have the best party ever. We have reason to celebrate tonight."

"You are a real trooper. I think you would want to go home and collapse."

"I could never do that, Jean-Luc. This gala and what it means to me is my raison d'etre. Let me sit here and catch my breath for a few minutes. Then we can go back and join the party and listen to Lynn entertain the guests. Just hold onto my arm. Please. I still feel a little wobbly on my pins."

49

Life began to settle. Before retiring, Penny contacted museums around the country to loan pieces of the exhibit for their collections.

The excitement was high at Hilltop. Lynn had just returned from a concert in Oslo and wasn't due to play her next show for another month. She welcomed the downtime.

Penny sat talking with Jean-Luc. "It was not the consequence I wanted. I prayed the police would find and prosecute Tennent, but the realization he is dead and no longer a threat, has freed me from my fear and anxiety. I can now walk down the street, shop, or go out to eat without looking over my shoulder. The old adage proves true, hatred can kill a man."

"It's the best alternate consequence I could ever think of," said Jean-Luc. "Let's go open that chilled bottle of champagne and enjoy some of Julie's hors d'oeuvres. We need to celebrate Lynn's homecoming and your retirement."

50

Ellen Worley stood next to her mother, Lynn; their heads turned upward, gazing at the campus building of Emerson College in Hollywood. Massive and modern, the glass and steel towered over Sunset Boulevard.

"Mom, did Penny attend college here?"

"Not at this campus, darling, she studied in Boston. That was the only campus at the time. Even though this magnificent structure was completed in 1986, it is considered young by Emerson standards. I had been in correspondence with the president of Emerson before Penny passed away last year. They wanted to honor Penny with a fountain or a statue in front of the Hollywood campus."

"That's a neat thing to do even if she graduated so many years ago. But why here and not in Boston?"

"I should have taken you to see the campus, then you would understand. There is no place the college could erect a fountain or a statue. It's right in the middle of downtown Boston. The Emerson board of directors voted to honor Aunt Penny after she donated the Driscoll wing to the Los Angeles County Museum of Art."

"Did you have to prepare a speech for today?"

"No, Ellen, this will be about a two-minute ceremony from start to finish."

"Look at the green tarps. It looks like they are covering something on the front sidewalk. Will there be chairs for us to sit in?"

"No, honey, there won't be chairs for us. And all I will be doing is thanking them for their gracious honoring of Penny. Your Dad should be here shortly. He promised to take us out for dinner. I'm looking forward to that. I'm too exhausted to set foot in the kitchen."

"I want lobster," Ellen informed her mother.

"We'll see." She quietly laughed at her fifteen-year-old daughter Ellen's exuberance.

"Lynn, Lynn, your remarks were beautiful. You should be so proud of yourself." Tom Worley crossed over to where his wife and daughter were standing. "I'm so sorry I wasn't standing next to Ellen while you were speaking. Traffic was awful from Pasadena. I took an Uber so we would only have one car." He ran his hand through his coiffed brown hair that had begun to show strands of silver.

Once the newspaper photographers took their shots and asked Lynn a few questions, they disappeared into the Friday night crowd. The plaza stood empty except for the Worley family.

"Daddy, did you videotape everything? Poor Aunt Trudy wasn't strong enough to come. I know she desperately wanted to be here." Ellen put her hands on her father's arm and gave him a big smile.

"Yes, I did, sweetheart. We will take the video to Hilltop this weekend. I know your aunt would love to see us and hear how you have progressed on the violin."

Lynn led the family back to where their car had been parked. "Ellen, would you mind if I sat in the back seat. I'm so tired. I just want to close my eyes for a bit. You can wake me at the restaurant. Ellen, darling, I'd like to play a duet with you. I have a request to play at a charity function, and it would be wonderful if we could show everyone how advanced you've become. Would you do that with me?"

Lynn laid her head back and closed her eyes.

Before Ellen could answer her mother, Tom looked at his wife through the mirror and saw she had drifted off to sleep. "Your mom must have had quite a day to close her eyes and fall asleep."

"She was wonderful, Daddy. I'd fall asleep too. She has been working so hard on this project. "Did the police ever catch that man, Tennent? I know Aunt Penny always traveled with a bodyguard. He hurt mom once, didn't he?"

"Yes, it was in San Francisco, her first significant concert. We think it was either Tennent or one of his cronies he paid to do it. I have been meaning to tell you that your mother and I talked about the violinist painting over the fireplace. Your mom brought it back from Berlin years ago, and it is quite a treasure. It seems fitting that you have that painting when you are older."

"I love that painting, the woman playing sort of looks like me. Tell me again about the time you and mom broke up."

"It was when Aunt Penny was in the hospital fighting for her life after a brutal knife attack."

"But the police caught him, didn't they? Didn't he die when he tried to hurt Aunt Penny at mom's concert in

L.A.?"

"Not exactly. Penny was hosting a gala at the museum with all the artwork she and your mom brought back from Berlin. Penny did most of the work labeling, counting, describing. It was the largest exhibition she had ever mounted before she retired. There was a receiving line, and guests were coming up to greet your aunt and to congratulate her. From out of nowhere, a man pulled out a revolver from beneath a huge bouquet of dark red roses and aimed it at Penny. He was raging and screaming and swearing at her but never got the chance to fire a bullet. The guy keeled over onto the marble floor and died of a massive heart attack. No, he's very much dead."

"Poor Aunt Penny. That must have been terrible for her. Tell me how you met mom. I'd love to know. Was it romantic?"

"I guess it was, but we almost didn't get married. In fact, we spend several years not even speaking to each other. That was after she broke off our engagement."

"Why did she do that?"

"I told her I wanted her to give up her career."

"Daddy, I would have told you no too."

"I know. That was when that scumbag Tennent

stabbed Aunt Penny."

"We didn't talk for several years, and then I saw her one night at a restaurant in Pasadena and asked her to have dinner with me. I could feel the icy air swirling around me, getting colder and colder as I stood next to her booth."

"Daddy, you're so dramatic."

Tom chuckled and continued his story. "By then, I had bought a small place of my own in Newport so that the trip wouldn't be far." He told his daughter.

"I said, 'Fine; I'll pick you up at seven on Friday evening.' She just about blew me away with the dress she was wearing. Your mom looked so gorgeous. We went for dinner at the Newport Harbor Yacht Club. Neither of us ate much. We just talked and talked and talked. By the end of the evening, I knew she was the girl for me. I always knew she was the girl for me. I think she felt the same way. I apologized profusely, repeatedly, for expecting her to put her career on hold for me. I was selfish and told her, 'you're a talented violinist, I won't ever stand in your way again and, I will support you in all your endeavors.'"

Tom held a reminiscent look. "We got married at Hilltop two weeks later, only four years after we had originally planned to do it. And you arrived ten months later."

"I'm so glad you're my Daddy."

"Me too, sweetheart. Me too."

Tom looked back at his sleeping wife again and smiled. "I think we're too late to have dinner at the Annandale. How about the Chop House? I know they have fish. Perhaps they will have your lobster."

Lynn slept while memories of years gone by flowed through her dreams.

Because of Penny Wells, Maud Driscoll's Legacy would remain untarnished and unbroken.

Lynn could hear violin music playing on forever.

Reviews

Book three: Alternate Consequence

ISBN: 978-0-9969593-8-4

"I had no idea a painting would lead to such death and destruction." That cogent summation of Judith Fabris' deliciously enticing new novel *Alternate Consequence* is a tempting morsel of the witty dialogue and globe-trotting mystery therein. Fabris takes us from Check-Point-Charlie in post- Cold-War Berlin (or is it) to the uber-chic art galleries of California in a tale rich with detail and delightfully executed. Murder has rarely been so much fun or so well choreographed, with violin score to boot.

David Eugene Perry,
Author of the award-winning
and critically acclaimed
mystery thriller,
Upon This Rock

Fabris does it again. She hooked me early on with the historical novel *Sargent's Lady*. I loved the story told through correspondence and the strong bond of friendship. Next, *The Missing Driscoll,* where excitement mounts as the author tackles an art forgery case. In *Alternate Consequence,* revenge reigns supreme as Fabris taunts us by resurfacing a nasty ex-con who thirsts for setting things right in his demented world. Like numbers one and two in this threequel, *Alternate Consequence* is a fascinating story. Fabris fans will delight as the saga continues.

Sunny Simon
Author, *Life on the Sunny Side*

Art curator and former owner of the Driscoll Art Gallery Penny Wells' grandmother, Maud Driscoll, was an internationally famous artist. Penny has a close circle of friends, all of whom have their own stories to tell. What Penny doesn't know is Bill Tennent has been released from prison after doing time for stealing a priceless Driscoll painting. Tennent is a vengeful man with Penny in his crosshairs.

Penny's friend Trudy King is the guardian of young Lynn Shepard, a promising violinist. Lynn learns she is the heir of a grand estate in East Germany belonging to her great uncle, Ernst Weber. Penny, Trudy, Ursula, Jean Luc, and others are on a quest accompanying Lynn to Germany to settle the estate and find some lost art. Lynn's great uncle had helped Jewish people escape the Nazis, and in gratitude, the Jews had left many valuable paintings and art objects with Ernst Weber, who had secreted them in the grand house, even in the walls.

While Lynn's friends are helping her sell the property, retrieving the lost pieces of art, and bringing them to a California art gallery, Bill Tennent embarks on a plan to kill Penny Wells. He plans first to get close to her through her inner circle. One of her friends has her throat slashed; another is murdered. Penny, herself, is brutally stabbed but survives. When Tennent learns in the newspaper he did not kill her, he becomes more determined and obsessed.

- Which one will be next on his list, and what will he do?

-Will this obsessed killer finally succeed with his revenge killing of Penny? How many will suffer his wrath before he finds his chance for revenge?

-Can the police protect Penny—any of them? Can they catch this murderer?

The author leads the reader through a tense drama and finishes with a stunning resolution, making *Alternate Consequence* an enjoyable and engrossing read.

Joanne Hardy
Author of *The Girl in the Butternut Dress*
and *Random Truths*

Book one: Sargent's Lady
ISBN: 978-0996843720

Sargent's Lady provides a satisfying prequel to *The Missing Driscoll* art mystery story and explores the life of Boston debutante Maud Driscoll, who finds herself alone and pregnant in Paris when her baby's father is murdered. As she cultivates her artistic talents, gives up her baby at birth, returns to America to a failed marriage and dreams, and goes back to Europe to find solace in painting once again, the rudiments of an artist's journey emerge.

The timeline moves from 1953 to 1889 and between Europe and America in a satisfying manner that is clarified by chapter headings identifying place and time. Readers are never left to wander or wonder, and will appreciate this clear approach to linking present-day affairs with choices of the past which resonate with consequences over time.

Judith Fabris does an especially notable job of exploring different characters in the story, from Maud's evolutionary process to Peter Wells, who buys a mysterious portrait in an art store, only to discover that its background story is even more surprising than he could ever have suspected. Forced by an art dealer to authenticate the subject of John Singer Sargent's undiscovered masterpiece, his probe into the past reveals an underlying story of sacrifice and survival that holds many astonishing connections to present-day family entanglements and history.

As the story winds through the years and juxtaposes Peter's search and revelations with his Aunt Maud's life, Paris comes to life in the course of a journey filled with unexpected revelations. Fabris takes time to build this sense of place, which is also a fine embellishment to the story line: *"A year later, Peter again found himself in Paris. It was July 14, Bastille Day, and Paris was celebrating on this warm summer day. He was enjoying his lunch at a sidewalk café, reminiscing how similar it was to the one where he had his first job. The pâté was excellent, and he savored the last bit of it spread on the remains of a baguette. He polished off the last cornichon, and squeezed the lemon rind into his expresso when a young woman stopped at his table."*

From a war which crushes communications between Europe and America and changes investigations and relationships both in families and in the art world, to Maud's winding journey away from art and back again, *Sargent's Lady* is a full-flavored story that will especially delight budding artists who like stories about the wellsprings of inspiration and life adversity: *"The colors also leapt off the canvasses Maud painted. She had been reborn. The smell of turpentine, and linseed oil were like the finest perfumes to her. Her studio, almost as large as the living room, was filled with easels and paints and paintings."*

The explorations of different generations changed by war and the contrasts between Maud Driscoll and Lillie Doty's experiences and lives is particularly thought-provoking and well-crafted as each cultivates different emotional reactions to adversity in their lives.

The result is a fine stand-alone story and a fitting companion to *The Missing Driscoll*. It's a tale of family ties, choices and consequences, war, and art that is highly recommended for its ability to live in the mind long after family affairs and artistic revelations are revealed.

D. Donovan
Senior Reviewer
Midwest Book Review

Book two: The Missing Driscoll

ISBN: 978-0996843768

Penny Wells is the museum curator at the Driscoll Museum, where her grandmother, artist Maud Driscoll, has her art on display. In *The Missing Driscoll*, Penny is invited to Paris to curate a Driscoll show of works from her museum, only to discover that one of the paintings is a forgery. But she personally supervised every step of the painting's preparation and shipping. How could a thief have gotten under the radar to make the swap on her watch?

As events progress, readers are treated to a globe-trotting art forgery case that involves Penny on a personal and professional level alike as her reputation is tarnished and she is forced to investigate the truth when a suspicious insurance adjustor suspects her of criminal activity.

It's refreshing to see an emphasis on the motivation for a non-sleuth to take up the reins to become an investigator. Penny had no inclination of developing her nose for trouble before these events and faces big challenges in pursuing the truth because her interests lie not in PI work, but in art.

She's a thirty-year-old unmarried woman whose passion, until now, has been relatively singular, but she also harbors strong family ties that are equally tested by tragedy and love. These family connections are also wound into the story and follow her footsteps as the insurance adjustor has an accident and the police become involved and questioning, as well.

Her pride in her museum role and her family heritage follow her throughout her experiences and inquiries. As Penny becomes convinced that Tennent was somehow involved, she curates new exhibits and waits for him to slip up somehow, even as she's drawn into the bigger mystery of Nazi history, art forgeries, and an evolving threat to her career and everything she loves.

The Missing Driscoll excels in strong characterization and a mystery that avoids predictability and reaches for the bigger picture in the art world, following Penny's journey through singular interests into a wider-reaching set of concerns that involves the global art community.

Its mystery is well done, intriguing, driven by several tragedies and personal ambition on all sides, and tinged with the promise of a romance Penny doesn't acknowledge or see coming. The question of not only whether she can find the missing Driscoll painting, but what happens when she does fuels a family-connected story that keeps readers engaged on more than one level.

Mystery enthusiasts who enjoy the art world and intrigue alike will find *The Missing Driscoll* an intriguing, well-crafted story with an international focus combined with many elements of the cozy mystery genre.

D. Donovan,
Senior Reviewer
Midwest Book Review

Judith Fabris

Judith Fabris is a lifelong writer who continues to explore many genres. She has a special imagination for designing plots and story lines. Her first published story appeared in her town newspaper when she was eight and when she saw her name in print, she was hooked. She wrote non- fiction until she became the caregiver for her husband who was very ill. An unintended consequence was the possibility of writing fiction where plotlines become fascinating stories. She has a talent for creating interesting characters and putting them in multi-layered plot lines. A native of California, Fabris lives in the low desert. When not traveling, she enjoys spending time with her family and friends. Be assured, her next novel will reflect new adventures.

Books by Judith Fabris

Sargent's Lady Series

    Book one: Sargent's Lady

    Book two: The Missing Driscoll

    Book three: Alternate Consequence

Kameleona (Hawaiian for Chameleon)

    A novel of redemption set on the island of Molokai

Non-Fiction

Money...Cool!

    Teach children about money and the stock market

Contact

judithfabris@yahoo.com

Amazon Author Central:

https://www.amazon.com/Judith-Fabris/e/B007OWQB8W

www.ingramcontent.com/pod-product-compliance
Lightning Source LLC
Chambersburg PA
CBHW022156260626
47155CB00019B/3057